**Love Released - Book Five
Of Women Of Courage
Love Released Serial**

By

Geri Foster

Thank You

Dear Reader,

Thank you for reading *Book Five of Women of Courage, Love Released*. I know venues are filled with many authors and books and the choices are limitless. I'm flattered that you choose my book. There are additional books in this series and if you enjoyed Cora and Virgil's journey, I hope you'll read the others.

If you'd like to learn when I publish new books, please sign up for my **Newsletter** www.eepurl.com/Rr31H. Again, I appreciate your interest and I hope you'll check out my other books.

Sincerely,
Geri Foster

Visit me at:

www.facebook.com/gerifoster1

www.gerifoster.com/authorgerifoster

www.gerifoster.com

Join us for discussion of Women of Courage @
https://www.facebook.com/groups/689411244511805/

Love Released
By Geri Foster

First Edition

Copyright 2015 by Geri Foster

ISBN-13: 978-1511837408

ISBN-10: 1511837403

Cover Graphics
Kim Killion
Lilburn Smith

Author contact information: geri.foster@att.net

This is a work of fiction. Names, characters, places, and incidents are either the product of the author's imagination or are used fictitiously. Any resemblance to actual persons living or dead, businesses, events, or locales is purely coincidental.

GERI FOSTER

ACKNOWLEDGEMENTS

This book dedicated to my husband, Laurence Foster. After all these years you're still my one and only love. Thank you for your support, and for believing in me when I had doubts. You've shown me that dreams really do come true and love isn't just in romance novels.

Always,

Geri Foster

CHAPTER ONE

Virgil, Ethan, Arthur, and Judge Garner headed toward the railroad tracks that separated the town. Once there, four cars and a pickup revved their engines. On the side of the road a burning cross, over seven feet tall, blazed hot in the evening shadows.

Virgil and his backup drove around the men dressed in white sheets and positioned themselves between the Ku Klux Klan and the colored community. JJ and a few others stood boldly to face the fanatical threat.

White robes flapping in the light breeze, the cowardly men hid their faces behind masks attached to the stupid looking conical hats. Holding his shotgun at his side, Virgil spit in disgust and stared them down. This kind of hate didn't belong in the world.

"You men clear out of Parker County. There's no place here for this kind of vigilante nonsense."

"You get out of our way, Sheriff. We came to hang Elmer Sparks for disrespecting a white woman on Main Street in Joplin three days ago."

"I don't care why you're here," Virgil shouted, his breath fogged in front of his face. "No one comes into my county and takes the law into his own hands."

"You bring him out here and we'll tend to him."

"I'll never turn a man over to a lynch mob." He cocked the double barrel shotgun. "But, I'll gladly blow a hole through anyone who lays a finger on one of my citizens."

"We demand justice and ain't no lawman gonna stand in our way."

"This one is."

"You notice you're out numbered," said the man behind the mask.

"You're standing in front of the best shots in this county or any other. Ethan here used to be a sniper in the military. He could take you all out in a few shots. I won't go into the rest of it, but if you have to hide behind a sheet, just how damned righteous are you?"

"That's none of your business and if you don't turn over Elmer Sparks we'll burn this whole damned town to the ground."

"You will when we're dead."

Touching the emblem on his chest, the leader shouted, "I'm the Grand Dragon of this here citizen's militia and you'd be smart to listen to what I say, boy."

JJ and several colored men came to the front of the line with weapons.

"What are they doing with guns?" The leader pointed his finger. "If you kill a white man, it'd be the end of your whole wretched neighborhood."

"No, it wouldn't," Judge Garner proclaimed. "If they shoot all of you, there won't be anyone left on your side to testify and we're damn sure not going to talk." The judge aimed his gun. "Grand Dragon, huh? Nothing grand about hiding in your mama's sheets."

Virgil nodded and Ethan threw a grenade under the front car. While they ducked, the whole front end of the Dodge flew into the air.

The leader jumped back, holding his hands up to protect his eyes. His cohorts cursed as they ducked from the flying debris. "What the hell do you think you're doing?"

Ethan bounced another grenade in his right hand. "You don't get out of here I'm going to blow up all these cars and every man in them."

Virgil stepped from behind his vehicle. "This town is in quarantine because we have an outbreak of influenza. You boys stick around much longer you might catch it."

The obvious leader said something to the men surrounding him. Muttering among themselves, several men tossed car parts into the bed of the pickup while others hooked the destroyed car to the bumper. Doors slammed, motors gunned and the caravan sped away.

Virgil turned. "Okay men, let's break this up and go back to our homes, you that can. Keep your weapons handy. I wouldn't put it past them to try to sneak back into town."

JJ shouldered his hunting rifle. "I thought we'd heard the last of that gang of tyrants with their bullying tactics."

Judge put his shotgun in the back seat of his car and said, "They're like this influenza. They crop up every once in a while. But with all the bad press they've been getting in the last few years, they don't have the power they used to."

Virgil was glad the situation had been defused for now. "We have other worries." He walked over to JJ. "How are things on your side of town?"

"We've lost a lot of people. I'm lucky no one from my family has taken sick, but my wife is helping out in the church. I worry about her night and day."

"Same with Cora. When Miss Winters brings Jack to stand outside the church, he begs her to come home. I know there's nothing else she'd rather do than be with her nephew."

JJ took Virgil by the arm and pulled him aside. "What have you heard from St. Louis?"

"I don't know if you noticed or not, but I've been really busy."

JJ tapped him on the chest. "You know what I'm talking about."

"I spoke to Batcher two days ago and he learned that Cora's estate was worth close to seventy thousand dollars."

JJ whistled. "That's a lot of money."

"Yeah, and her defense cost less than five thousand."

Looking around, JJ shrugged. "So, where's her money?"

"Apparently her father took it."

"Really?" He looked toward the judge. "Does she know that?" he asked shaking his head as Virgil put his weapons away.

"Not yet."

CHAPTER TWO

It had been sixteen days since the outbreak when Virgil and Cora had gone into the church to tend to the sick. After two days without a casualty, no new patients and no one running a fever, Virgil, Ethan, Maggie, Helen, Mae, the judge and Cora stood on the steps of the church while the people of Gibbs City applauded them.

The last victim had been John, Virgil's deputy, who'd worked so hard to help those in the church. When they brought in his sick girlfriend and she died, John started running a fever later that day. He was gone by the following nightfall.

Over eighty Gibbs City residents had lost their lives despite all the hard work and efforts of those who'd cared and tried to save as many as possible.

Still, hundreds had made it through the worst part. Today the sun broke through the dark clouds and Cora lifted her face to the warmth. They'd made a difference.

Earl had survived despite the odds, but the sickness had left him weak and unable to care for himself. Luckily, Miss Winters had been doing double duty until he regained his strength.

Cora knelt down and opened her arms and Jack ran toward her as fast as his little legs would carry him. Pal ran right beside him barking and wagging his tail. He must've been happy to see her as well.

Once in her arms, Cora squeezed her nephew and thanked God for delivering them from the grips of influenza. Taking Jack's hand, they walked home, a smile on her face. Things could finally get back to normal and, hopefully, no more people would die.

Inside the house, Virgil slumped on the couch. "I never thought I'd say this felt good, but it does right now."

The table and countertops were covered with casserole dishes neighbors had brought so she wouldn't have to cook. "This is all very thoughtful. I'm heating one up for dinner."

Standing on his tip-toes, Jack eyed all the food. "As long as I don't have to eat Miss Winters' cooking ever again." He curled up his nose. "Earl's right, that woman can't boil water."

Those were words straight out of her neighbor's mouth. "That's a rude thing to say about someone who's been taking good care of you for the last two and a half weeks. Miss Winters is very nice."

"Oh, she's nice all right, but that don't mean she can cook."

Virgil stood and laughed. He put his hand on Jack's bony shoulder. "You know what our problem is, son?"

Shaking his head, Jack looked up at Virgil. "Your Aunt Cora has us spoiled. She can make anything taste good."

The young boy thought about that for a while, then nodded. "Yeah, I think you're right, Uncle Virgil. We've got the best cook in the county."

Cora inwardly smiled. Her two guys were sure in love with her talents in the kitchen. She turned on the oven and put a macaroni dish in and closed the door. Looking for something she thought Earl would like, she settled on a dish of scalloped potatoes and ham. "I'm taking this next door. He's still too weak to get around very well. I've asked Miss Winters to look after him for a couple of more weeks."

Virgil went about setting the table. "Good luck to her. Earl's so cantankerous I'm surprised she puts up with it."

After donning a sweater, Cora knocked on her neighbor's door then went inside. The changes brought her to a staggering halt. The messy, cluttered rooms were now spotless and well organized. Earl sat in his easy chair with his feet propped up.

"How are you?" she asked. "The color is coming back to your face."

"I'm doing okay if you'll get rid of that pestering old woman."

Placing the dish in the oven, Cora looked around. "From what I can see, it seems she's doing a remarkable job. I wouldn't be in such a hurry for her to leave, if I were you."

"Why the hell not?"

Cora spread out her hands. "Just look. The house is clean, your clothes are freshly washed and I see you have some new kitchen curtains."

"She did that, the old bat."

Sitting on the couch across from Earl, Cora gave him her sharpest scowl. "Earl, you're kicking a gift horse in the mouth. Miss Winters has done a good job of looking after you and Jack. That's a lot to ask of a woman her age."

"Then don't ask her. Tell her I don't need her anymore."

"But you do. You're still weak and I feel better if there's someone looking after you."

Earl scowled. "She's a pain."

"You should be grateful."

"Why?"

"Because you have someone to care for you. She even does the cooking."

"She can't cook."

"She's better than Meredith."

"Hell, I'm better than Meredith."

"Earl it's just until you get better, then she can resume her normal life. She's only doing it as a favor to me."

"Then take that damned favor and be done with it."

"Be nice. You could've ended up in the hospital."

"She's done nothing but clean."

Cora could understand why. Earl's house had needed a good cleaning for years. No way on God's green earth would she remind him that this was the first time she'd ever seen his hair combed.

If she didn't know better she'd think there could be something between the two of them. Evelyn was sure a lot happier and more chipper lately.

Earl insisted she help him to her house so he could eat dinner with them, so she put the casserole in the icebox for another day. She didn't want him out in the cold, but she imagined he was sick of being cooped up in the house for days.

Virgil set another plate out when she and Earl sat down. "What's up?"

She was so exhausted after their ordeal she could barely hold her head up. All she wanted to do was sleep for two days. Same for Virgil. He'd been groggy all day. She honestly didn't think they would've lasted much longer.

"I'm sure glad all this is over with," her neighbor said. "I've miss having Missy around."

"So have I," Jack said. "I don't never want anything bad to come to town again."

Virgil spooned out the casserole while Cora sliced the bread. "No one does. We've had our fair share of trouble."

Just as Cora picked up her fork, a knock sounded at the back door. Virgil answered and stepped back. Reverend Fuller entered the kitchen, his hat in his hand. "I don't want to bother you, Miss Williams, but I was wondering if I might have the list of names you kept track of."

He referred to those who'd died. "Yes, it's in here." He didn't move and she looked at the unshaven, doe-eyed man and her heart squeezed. "Reverend Fuller have you had dinner?"

He held up his hands. "Oh, no, ma'am I don't want to disturb your family."

Virgil took another plate from the cupboard. "Nonsense, we've more food than we could ever eat. Take a seat."

Jack ran and dragged in an extra chair from the back porch and pushed it to the table. Fuller looked around before slowly lowering himself onto the seat. Cora took his hat and hung it on the back porch hook while Virgil helped him off with the suitcoat he'd been wearing since the day he staggered back into the church to help.

Fuller held out his palms. "Mind if I wash my hands?"

She pointed to the faucet. "Of course not. Help yourself to the sink."

Cora took her place at the table and scooted her chair closer. She and Earl exchanged puzzled looks, but she could tell by Virgil's sharp eyes he was guarded and unconvinced the reverend had seen the light.

When Fuller joined them, he smiled for the first time in days. "This looks delicious."

"It's much better than the sandwiches we were surviving on all those days at the church," Virgil said.

"Mrs. Welsh brought this over so I wouldn't have to cook tonight. I must say, I'm very grateful."

"We're all grateful, Miss Williams." Reverend Fuller lowered his head. "We're grateful that you were kind enough to step in and help Gibbs City when we needed you the most."

She placed her hand on his shoulder. "You brought a lot of comfort to those in their darkest hour, Reverend."

He looked beseechingly at Earl. "I hope I can continue to be of service to this community."

Cora's neighbor picked up his cup and took a sip. "That's something Arthur and I will be talking about."

Heads were lowered to give thanks for being together. With a deep sigh, they all enjoyed a meal together for the first time in weeks. After Earl and Reverend Fuller left, Cora took her time getting Jack ready for bed. School resumed tomorrow and he was excited to be seeing all his friends.

Virgil came in when she was pulling the blanket up around the happy, little boy. "You sleep tight, Jack. Tomorrow things return to normal."

Snuggling deeper into the covers, Jack giggled. "I know, now if it will just snow."

They left the room. Cora pulled the door partly closed. "I can do without any more cold weather."

"It's not even Thanksgiving yet. There's a whole lot more snow on the way."

She poured them a cup of coffee and sat at the kitchen table enjoying the peace and quiet of her own home. Virgil reached across and touched her hand. "Do you know how much money you were worth before prison?"

Pulling from his grasp, she turned aside, not wanting to get all tangled in the past. "That's not important."

"Yes, it is."

She shrugged. "I have no idea."

"Pretty close to seventy thousand dollars."

Anger flared in her stomach and she tightened her jaw. "How did you come across that bit of information?"

He cocked his head. "Do you know how much was spent on your defense?"

Glaring, she shook her head. "I don't, but I'm sure you do."

"A little under five thousand."

The air swooshed from her lungs and a giant fist slammed into her chest. "What?" she gasped. "How much did you say?"

"You had all that money and your father hired the most inexperienced lawyer for the least amount of money he could find." As if sensing her pain, he captured her hands. "Why would he do that?"

She pulled her hands away from him. Her head spun and her vision blurred. Twisting her hands in in her lap, she shook her head in despair. The thought of her father's betrayal never stopped surprising her. "I don't know."

"If you'd had a half-decent attorney you wouldn't have spent a day behind bars. Your father deliberately sent you to prison. He not only didn't lift a finger to help you, he did everything in his power to see the deed done."

Tears stung her eyes and Cora struggled to breathe. She stood, tipping the chair over. Fury balled her fists. "You went to St. Louis to find out about my past didn't you?"

He lowered his gaze. "Yes."

CHAPTER THREE

Virgil hated causing Cora pain. No doubt the words coming from his mouth cut like a knife, inflicting enormous agony. It hurt him as much as her. "It's not what you think."

"Oh," she stepped back, her small hands trembling. "Now you claim to know my thoughts. What a talented man."

"I didn't go there out of my own curiosity. Judge Garner sent me. He's the one who wanted answers."

"Why?" she pleaded. "That can only lead to trouble for me and Jack. Why can't people leave us alone?"

"It's the prison, Cora. An innocent man was murdered. Inhuman things are being done to people behind those walls. And now Becker is threatening to put you back in prison."

"What?" she staggered backwards, her hands on her chest. "You can't be serious. I have my release papers." Wouldn't that keep her out of prison? They'd set her free.

Taking two steps toward her, Virgil reached out and gripped her arms. "I know that, but you were released before your discharge date. A month early. He can get a judge to make you go back and serve that time."

"I can't! I can't go back there."

"That's what the judge and I are trying to prevent from happening. I'd rather lose my right arm than for you to be subjected to that nightmare again."

She looked around. "Jack? What will happen to him?"

"Nothing because we're not going to let it."

"But you can't stop Becker, or Judge Martin, or even my father. Those are mean, powerful men who would kill an honest, decent man like you without blinking an eye."

"Why did your father want you in prison?"

"I don't know that, Virgil. I know he was always angry because I became a doctor. It annoyed him that I didn't marry well and we've clashed since I was a teenager. But, to my knowledge, I've never done anything that would warrant him wanting to put me away."

"Except you shot Dan Martin."

She turned and paced the small kitchen as she nibbled her fingernails. "I went to my father and told him that I'd gone to the hospital and it appeared Eleanor hadn't committed suicide. I told him I thought Dan had murdered her."

"What did he say? Describe the event exactly like it happened."

"He'd been drinking. I heard my mother sobbing from the corner of his study. Jack was still at the Martins." She went to the living room and grasped the back of the couch as if looking for support. "He told me I was making wild accusations. He chided me for saying such things in front of my mother."

"So he didn't believe you?"

Her brows wrinkled. "I don't think he wanted to believe it, or maybe didn't want to hear the truth. But he never denied my claim."

"What did you do?"

"I'd had a problem with a break-in a few months earlier so I'd gone to a pawnshop and bought a pistol for protection." She wrung her hands. "I was angry that no one was willing to fight for Eleanor. No one cared enough to see that Daniel Martin got what he deserved."

"So, you got the gun and went to his home?"

Tears ran down her cheeks and she brushed them away. "Yes. I was blinded by anger and rage."

"What happened at the Martin's house?"

"Eleanor and Dan lived with his parents in their mansion. So I went there. The maid let me in because I'd been there so many times before."

"Who was there?"

"I went into the family room and Dan's mother sat on a small chair puffing on a long cigarette relaxing, acting as if nothing had happened. They were clearly dressed for a dinner party but Dan's father, Albert, was clearly disturbed about something."

"The judge?"

"Yes."

"Dan, on the other hand, had on a clean shirt and pants." She looked away. "I noticed blood on his left shoe. I imagined it was Eleanor's." Cora fought back tears, but still they flowed down her cheeks. "I was so angry."

"At Dan?"

"At all of them. No one, not even my own family, seemed to care that a wonderful, loving mother was dead. Murdered as if her life meant nothing. The Martins acted like it was all an inconvenience. Messy and socially unacceptable."

"Were they there when you shot Dan?"

"No. The judge and his wife had an affair to attend. On the way out, Dan's mother said she wasn't going to stand around listening to some hysterical woman carry on so crassly."

"So you and Dan were alone?"

"Yes, it happened in his father's study."

"What did Dan say when you accused him of murder?"

"He actually looked to the door as if hoping his father would come back and get him out of a jam."

"You didn't like Jack's father?"

"Not especially. He was just a rich kid who was nothing without the influence of his father."

"No job?"

She chuckled harshly. "Are you kidding? The man never lifted a finger in his life. Even managed to get kicked out of Princeton."

The tension grew quieter as Cora settled down. She'd never admitted this much to him before and Virgil was thankful so many things were cleared up. The one constant was that Cora should've never gone to prison. And her father could've prevented the entire thing from happening.

Virgil pulled her into his arms. She came reluctantly, but at last he managed to have her warm body pressed against his. The epidemic had taken its toll on him. He was physically and mentally exhausted and he knew the same was true for Cora.

Losing John had left Virgil with an emptiness he didn't expect. While he and John weren't the closest of friends, they'd worked together from the beginning and Virgil had known him all his life.

Tomorrow they would start burying the dead.

Looking down at Cora's tear-filled, brown eyes, he picked her up in his arms and walked toward the bedroom. He slowly undressed her, leaving on her undergarments then, after taking off his pants and shirt, he crawled into bed, pulled her close and fell into a deep healing sleep.

CHAPTER FOUR

When Jack woke them up, Cora was surprised to find Virgil lying next to her, still sleeping. "It's time to get ready for school, Aunt Cora."

She quickly dressed while Jack brushed his teeth. If he found it strange that Virgil was in her bed, he didn't say anything. Hopefully, he wouldn't repeat the incident at school.

With a hairbrush in hand, she shook Virgil awake. He rolled over and yawned. "What time is it?"

"Jack saw us in the bed together. I hope he doesn't say anything."

Virgil rubbed the sleep from his eyes. "I don't think he will."

Pressed for time, Cora quickly made oatmeal for breakfast, fried some bacon and perked a pot of coffee. Virgil came out and took a seat next to Jack who was leaning on his hand, a sad look on his face.

"What's wrong?" Virgil asked.

"It's not snowing."

He turned around and glanced out the kitchen window. "That doesn't mean it won't later today."

"I wanted to walk in the snow today."

"There will be plenty of those days before winter is over."

"I sure hope so. I want to build another snowman. Don't you, Uncle Virgil?"

Virgil laughed. "That was a lot of fun. We'll do it again soon. But for now, you better eat up. Maggie and Tommy will be here soon for school."

He finished breakfast and ran out the door when Tommy banged on the back door. Cora leaned out and waved at her friend then she sat down for a cup of coffee. "I feel like I could sleep a week."

Virgil ate a piece of bacon. "Me too, but I've got too much to do today. Lots of families will be making funeral arrangements, and some will stop by to give their condolences over John."

She put her hand on his, knowing his pain. "I'm so sorry, Virgil. I know how much he meant to you."

"I'll miss him, but so many lost so much more. I almost feel guilty mourning."

"Yes, the poor Nelson's lost all five of their children. Such a tragedy."

He reached over and kissed her. "I'll see you later today."

Cora cleaned the kitchen then left for the dry cleaners. Inside, her friends greeted her enthusiastically. But one friend, Helen, was missing. She was still getting over the loss of her husband, Don, and Arthur had insisted she take some time off.

Nell met her as she opened the counter. "What are you doing here?"

"I'm back to work."

Arthur came from the adjoining room. "Didn't Earl tell you?"

"Tell me what?"

"That the hospital board is considering taking steps to reinstate your medical license. They want to offer you a job." He took out his pocket watch. "You're due at the hospital in an hour."

"What?"

Nell waved a towel at her. "Get moving."

"Wait." Cora rehashed Arthur's words. Could it be true?

"For what."

"I'm not sure I want that."

"Cora, this is your chance to get back to what you've loved doing."

"But I have Jack."

Arthur put his hand on her shoulder and looked deeply into her eyes. "Plenty of successful people have kids. Help them to understand that you don't want to work long hours or any of that stuff. Do it your way."

She waved goodbye then hurried to the hospital. Dr. Lowery met her in the main lobby and took her upstairs to a conference room where Ben, Earl, Dr. Westley, JJ, and Dr. Chesterfield from St. Louis waited.

"I wasn't made aware of any of this. I'm sorry to be so unprepared."

The judge frowned. "We made a mistake by leaving it up to Earl to notify you to be here."

Dr. Westley cleared his throat. "What we'd like to do is apply to get your license back. You've helped this community and you've been someone we all admire. The people in this room are willing to put in a good word for you with the State Board. We just need to know if you want it."

"I do. I love helping people, but I don't want it to become my life. I now have a child to raise and he's my main priority."

"We can work with that," Dr. Lowery said. "Pick your own hours."

Cora closed her eyes and imagined returning to what she loved. Her heart quickened. "That would be lovely."

"Or you could start your own office and hang out a shingle."

Cora shook her head. "Oh, that's too demanding and I don't want to do that."

Dr. Chesterfield opened a folder. "Well, I think we need to get down to business."

Cora reached over and squeezed his arm. He'd been a good friend and a man she admired. "Thank you for coming, Dr. Chesterfield."

He patted her hand and smiled. "My pleasure."

"Dr. Chesterfield, you worked the longest with Miss Williams. What do you have to say?"

"She's a great physician and really cares about people. She's smart and willing to try new things. I think she'd be a wonderful addition to any hospital. I'd know I'd love to have her back in St. Louis."

Cora shook her head. "I don't' want to go there. My life is here in Gibbs City." She thought about Virgil. This was exactly where she wanted to live and being a doctor was exactly what she wanted to do.

Could this dream be possible? What if she got her hopes up and it didn't happen?

Benjamin Welsh, the druggist stood. "Cora is the most compassionate person I know. Not because she gave us Ronnie, but because she cared enough to get involved and make sure he was safe at the risk of her own life."

Earl tapped his cane. "I have nothing but good to say about, Missy. This place has been a little rough on her, but despite that, she's been remarkably kind. After spending time with her in the church while she cared for the sick and dying, I think she's a good doctor."

Dr. Westley spoke. "She saved a young, colored girl because she couldn't walk away from someone suffering. And she could've and no one would've said a word. But she didn't. She insisted the child be cared for in this very hospital. No doubt she has the necessary compassion."

When Cora left, she couldn't feel her feet touching the ground. They would all recommend to the state that she be reinstated and they'd know in a couple of days. In the meantime, she went to Virgil's office to give him the good news. If he already knew, she was going to choke him.

It turned out he was as surprised as she was and as delighted. They went for lunch at Betty's Diner and enjoyed a hamburger. They were both hopeful all would go well.

Cora couldn't wipe the smile from her face. "Wouldn't that be wonderful?"

"It's what you are, Cora. How can it not be the best thing to happen?"

"I can't wait to find out." She took his hand. "I can't help but fear that somehow my father will get his hands into this and keep it from happening."

"Why would he even want to?"

She looked away. "I don't know why he hates me. At first I thought it was because I went to medical school against his wishes, but now it seems to be so much more."

"Maybe because you shot Daniel Martin. Would that have embarrassed him?"

She shrugged. "I don't see why. I mean, he didn't like Dan any more than I did. Eleanor had done exactly as expected for him and our mother. She married a rich man from a powerful family. She gave him a grandson, stayed home and created a perfect, family life and entertained elegantly."

"While you went out to heal the sick and save mankind?"

"I had a very good life. I made a lot of money, I didn't need them for anything and I was determined to never marry."

"Then you shot Dan Martin and your father hired the worst attorney in the state?" Virgil took a drink of coffee. "He told you that your defense cost every dime you had. I heard him."

"I know, but he's a very wealthy man, he doesn't have to steal from me, so why would he?"

"Who hired your attorney?"

"My father. He was a long-time, family acquaintance."

"Do you feel he did you justice?"

She took a sip of iced tea. "No, I went to prison."

"Did he try to save you?"

"No, not really. I thought maybe he was so confident they would dismiss the case that he felt little reason to put up a full defense."

"What did he think when you were sentenced to prison?"

"He was disappointed."

"Not surprised?"

She held a fry in the air. "I don't think he was that surprised."

"You know that was all part of the plan, don't you?"

"It didn't take me long to realize that the whole thing was a travesty and that Judge Martin was out to get me for shooting his precious son."

"The man didn't even go to a doctor."

"No, but I think, like my father, Judge Martin wanted to make a point. Also, it shut me up. I accused his son of murdering my sister. That didn't sit too well."

"Do you think he put you in prison to make sure his son didn't face charges?"

She shoved her plate aside. "I'm sure of it."

"Tell me one thing. Your father is an influential man. Lots of connections and money. Why would he allow Judge Martin to put his daughter in prison?"

She moved her gaze to the window. "I don't know."

"It doesn't make sense. Yes, he was probably angry you became a doctor instead of a debutante. But no father would go to that extreme because he didn't like the direction his kid's life went."

"It's confusing."

"Did your father and Judge Martin do business together?"

She looked at him sharply. "When you went to St. Louis you investigated the reason I was sent to prison." Anger flared her nostrils even though she'd known it all along. "You went to spy on my past."

"I did what I was told to do. I didn't go there on my dime. I told you, Judge Garner sent me."

"You don't see that as a betrayal to me?"

"What, wanting to learn what had happened to you so I could figure out why your father went to the Missouri State Penitentiary for Women to see the warden?"

She leaned back, pressing against the vinyl booth. "What are you talking about?"

"Your father visited the prison on several occasions."

"Who told you that?"

"First, Ted Young hinted to it. Then a snitch Judge Garner had in the pen told him."

"I can hardly believe that. Why would my father go there and yet never visit me?"

"Those are the answers I'm looking for."

The outside world spun and Cora struggled to get her balance. "So, he had to know, or at least suspect, the things they did to me."

"I'd guess that's correct."

Until now, she thought her father couldn't hurt her anymore because she didn't love him. But to learn he allowed those savages to completely break her like a shattered glass, crushed her chest and made her physically ill. Her stomach churned and the tempo of her heart throbbed at her temples.

The absolute betrayal.

He could've saved her and yet he chose not to. Despair swamped Cora until she felt suffocated. Pushing away from the booth, she ran all the way home sobbing. In the safety of her room, she fell across her bed shivering. Why? Why would he do that to her?

The door opened and she knew it was Virgil by the steady pace of his footsteps that carried him into her bedroom where he laid down beside her and drew her to his chest.

"I never knew he hated me so much."

"I'm sorry, Cora. I'm sorry about all this. I didn't want to hurt you. I'd never do that. But, I do want to kill your father."

She rolled over and faced him. "I guess, deep in my heart, I wanted him to love me, craved his approval, but not like Eleanor. My sister would've moved heaven and earth to make my parents proud of her. And they were, just not enough to insist her murderer be brought to justice."

CHAPTER FIVE

Virgil entered his office where he found Ethan and a mountain of food piled on John's old desk. "I see it's getting worse. You might as well take that home to your family because Cora's kitchen is full of food, too."

"I know. In times like this, people don't know what to do so they just bring food. I appreciate your offer. If there's one thing my tribe of three kids can do, it's eat."

"I imagine so with two growing boys. I'm glad your family managed to escape the flu outbreak."

"Every time that door opened, I feared it would be one of my kin. My heart practically jumped out of my chest with worry."

After pushing aside several dishes, Virgil sat on the edge of the desk. "Now that John's gone, I was wondering if you'd want the Deputy job full-time. The pay's good and you'll probably have better hours than at the foundry."

"I've been thinking on that and I like the idea. This way I might get to spend a little time with my children."

"That's what I was thinking. The job's yours if you want it. I've already had it approved by the County Commissioners."

Ethan held out his hand. "I appreciate the offer."

"Anything else going on?"

"Not a single thing. Most people are trying to get back to living a normal life. Some are struggling because they weren't able to work for so long with most of the businesses closed."

"Yeah, that's always an additional burden."

Ethan cocked his hip. "Several have come by to see if I need any help in my repair business, but people have other things on their minds besides remodeling or repairing."

"We heard today that Cora may get her medical license back."

The outer door banged as the judge hurried in. "We're hearing good things back from the State Board about that," he said. "They're seriously considering reinstating her."

"Good to see you, Judge." Virgil patted the older man on the shoulder. "She'll be proud to hear that."

"It's just a matter of the paperwork coming through. Once that's done, she can start practicing again."

Ethan stepped forward. "She worked awfully hard trying to save as many people as she could."

The judge ran his hand around the rim of his hat. "Speaking of, have you heard from Reverend Fuller?"

"No, he stopped by Cora's for dinner last night, took the list of those who'd lost loved ones then left."

"I got a call from Arthur today saying several citizens had called to tell him Fuller had been by to offer the families of those deceased all the help he could. He'll be presiding over most of the funerals."

"Well, he sure turned a corner."

"I guess he's taken Edith's body to Joplin where she'll be buried near her family. I'm wondering if Arthur and Earl still plan to get rid of him."

"I can't say. Maybe they're just waiting to see how it goes. Right now the town needs to come together and share the grief they're suffering. Friends and family mean a lot."

"No doubt about that." Taking out his pocket watch, the judge flipped the cover and checked the time. Snapping it shut, he stuck it back in his pocket. "I have court in fifteen minutes so I better get a move on."

"See you," Virgil called out.

"I'm awfully glad the epidemic is all over." Ethan looked out the window as Caroline Dixon walked by. "She was sure a lot of help, too."

"This town has depended on her family for a long time. She took right up where her father left off."

Ethan shook his head. "Can't say the same about her mother."

"No, Josephine is too selfish and self-centered. And with that new husband of hers, it's kind of sad to see the way she disrespects Big Jim's name."

"Caroline more than makes up for that."

Ethan asked, "Will you be leaving for St. Louis again?"

"I don't know. The DA is thinking about opening an investigation about what's going on inside the prison. If he does that, then I might have to return. I hope not. Cora hates it when I'm away."

"You're probably not too happy, either."

"No, I have no love for St. Louis."

"Neither do I. Never have."

With so many funerals to organize over the next three days, Ethan headed out to help the undertaker. Virgil rubbed the sleep from his eyes. Hanging his coat on the rack by his office door, he slumped into his old, office chair. Exhaustion weighed down his shoulders. Sighing, he picked up the phone to call David Batcher when his father walked in.

"What are you doing in town?"

"Just dropping by to see how you're doing. I know you've been really busy with the epidemic."

"I'm just glad you and mom weren't part of it." Virgil shook his head. "So many died."

"I know, your mother and I lost several friends we've known most of our lives. I imagine we'll be busy the next few days attending funerals."

"It's all been horrible."

His father adjusted the chair in front of his desk then sat down and folded his arms. "You spoke to me some time ago about my filling station. I came into town to pay the yearly taxes and thought I'd see if you wanted to continue that discussion."

"Buford and Carl are both really good mechanics, Dad. And I was hoping they could buy the place from you. Or maybe lease it for the time being."

"Like I told you, it takes a lot of money just to get it started and you've got stiff competition."

"Off the top of your head, how much do you figure they'd need?"

"Depends on the price of gas."

"I'm wondering if the bank will loan them the money."

"You can see, but I don't know how I feel about Carl being in anything." His father fidgeted in the chair. "I've expressed to you before that he's not reliable."

"I know, but I think if he had something to do, he'd get better." His father's tight lips signaled his doubt. "I know Carl's reputation, but I also know that deep down inside, he's a good man."

Roy Carter shook his head. "I have no qualms about Buford. He's a good worker. But do either of them have a business head?"

"I doubt it. I just thought you have the building sitting there collecting dust. You pay yearly taxes on an empty station. I just thought maybe you might want to get it off your hands."

"I tried to sell it when I retired, but no one made an offer."

"So what would you have to lose if Carl and Buford made you an offer?"

"First, I'd want them to pay the tax bill, and fill up the tanks. If they can manage that, I'll help some. Now, I ain't saying I'll float the whole thing, but I'm willing to give them a try."

Virgil smiled. "Let me talk to Buford and Carl. I'll see what we can come up with."

"If they can make money on the business, I'll eventually sell them the building and the contents. I'm sure we can come up with good terms for all of us."

"Can you help them out in the business part? Show them how to keep the books, take in the cash and stuff like that?"

"I don't have anything better to do, but this is a bad time to go into business."

"It's winter, people need tires, batteries and gasoline," Virgil pointed out.

"Well, see what you can find out and let me know. Briggs at the bank might be a good place to start."

"He's new at the job and could be reluctant to take chances."

"He's also fair and believes in building up this community. And you don't know until you ask."

Virgil and his father decided to have coffee and pie at Betty's Diner. They sat in the back booth reminiscing about those who'd passed when Reverend Fuller stumbled through the door.

He'd cleaned up and changed clothes, but the circles under his eyes indicated that he hadn't slept in days and he looked like he'd dropped a few pounds. Probably still grieving over his dead wife.

Virgil called him over. "Reverend, come and sit with us."

He moved warily in their direction. When he reached the booth he held out his hand to Virgil's father. "I'm glad to see you made it through the sickness, Mr. Carter."

"Have a seat," Virgil said.

"I just dropped by for a sandwich before going back to the undertaker's. I'm helping with the families of those with loved ones to bury." He shook his head. "It's very difficult for them."

"Ethan is there as well."

"Yes, he came in just as I left. I went home expecting Edith to be there with lunch, but she's gone." He stared at the tabletop, sad and half-dead himself. Grief was a powerful thing.

"I'm aware of that. Did you get her buried?"

"Yesterday was the funeral. With so many people wrapped up in their own sorrow only a few attended, but I was grateful for all that were there."

"How'd her family take it?"

Rubbing a trembling hand over his haggard face, he let out a deep, sorrowful breath. "They blamed me." He looked away. "I can't say I fault them for that. I wasn't much of a husband."

Virgil's father spoke. "We can't relive mistakes, Charles. It only makes us sad. God has a purpose."

The waitress came and took their order. Lost in misery, the reverend stayed quiet through the meal, then paid and left. Virgil tried to imagine what he'd feel if he had lost Cora from the sickness. His gut twisted and tears stung his eyes.

He wouldn't be able to go on, either.

CHAPTER SIX

Pal barked before the knock sounded at the front door. Cora peeked outside and saw JJ standing on the porch with a big grin on his face. She immediately invited him. Her heart thudded loudly in her chest as she wondered if she dared hope for another chance.

"The State Board has contacted us back and you're fully reinstated."

Grabbing him by the shoulders, she screamed with joy and pulled JJ against her for a big hug. He squeezed her and they danced around the living room with Pal yapping frantically and joining in their celebration.

She stopped and held on to his arms. "What did they say?"

"It appears the ruling wasn't really sanctioned by the State Board. Judge Martin's name was all over that complaint. Your father's as well. But there hadn't been a true ruling that your license be revoked."

She shook her head. "It's amazing isn't it? How they can hate me so much."

"No, it's not amazing to me. Those are two evil men who have no goodness in their hearts at all. That's why my mother hated your father and stayed away from him."

"I miss Aunt Rose. I mostly miss her wisdom during times like these when she always knew the right thing to do. Now, I feel lost. I'd like to confront my father, but at the same time I want to stay so far away from him that I never have to look at his face again."

"I can understand. And I feel sorry for Jack. He'll never know either grandparent. Not even his father."

"I don't want him to know those vicious people."

JJ opened his briefcase and handed her a medical certificate. "Here's the temporary paper. The others will come in the mail. I have to get to court."

JJ closed the door behind him and Cora stared at the document in her shaking hands. Her whole life was summed up on a piece of paper.

Raising her eyes, she looked around. This little house was her identity. It was full of warmth and love and Jack and Virgil and Pal. Friends sat at her table and she loved the life she and Jack had created.

There was nothing out there that meant as much as right here in her heart. Home, love, family, friends. In one's life nothing came close to that. A job, even a career was wonderful, but it would always lead her back here.

Home.

Power surged through her body and she felt so validated she wanted the world to know. She called Dr. Chesterfield and the others who were at the meeting and thanked them for helping her and putting in a good word.

Then she called her father. The phone rang three times before Naomi answered. "Tell my father I'm on the phone, Naomi, and I want to speak to him."

"I'm not sure he'll take the call, Cora. You know how stubborn he can be."

"Ask him anyway."

Soon her father's booming voice traveled to her ear. "What do you want?"

"Just to tell you that despite all your efforts and those of your cronies, I have my license back and I can practice medicine. I'm also a well-respected member of this community."

"How did you manage that?"

"I was a decent person. I didn't set out to destroy anyone and I love those close to me. Something you've never understood."

"I spoke to the State Board myself and they said you'd never be a doctor again."

"You shouldn't underestimate the power of good people with good intentions."

"Go ahead and gloat. I don't care. Your mother and I are through with you."

"You've been through with me for years, but I must ask, where is all my money you stole?"

"I didn't steal your money."

"I was worth close to seventy thousand dollars and my defense only cost five. What did you do with the rest? Pay off the judge? And don't forget all the other corrupt people you used to put your own daughter in prison where she was tortured every day."

"Don't be so dramatic. You weren't tortured."

Cora stopped as confusion set in. Her mind rehashed her harsh treatment. "My life was a mental, physical and emotional hell every single day I was there. Not just because I was in prison, but the things they did to me were merciless. They put me in a coffin and nailed it shut for days." She sucked in a great gulp of air. "Days that I was frightened, alone, hungry, and desperate. They treated me like an animal and you let them."

She slammed down the phone and wiped away the tears. That, she vowed, would be the last time she'd ever speak to her father again.

Waiting for her nerves to settle before calling Virgil with the good news, she looked over and saw Earl, her neighbor, at the back door. She invited him to come in and then she put on a pot of coffee. He looked better every day, but not as good as she wanted him to because of his battle with influenza.

"How's it going at your house today?" she asked. "I noticed Evelyn is over there."

He looked disgusted. "Cleaning like a fiend."

"She probably wants to make sure you're comfortable."

"She's a damned nuisance."

"Well, soon you'll be on your own if you keep getting better."

"It damn sure won't be because of her cooking."

"It sure is something. You're gaining weight, your color is good and you look nice and well-groomed."

"I can look any damned way I want. I have to get dressed every day because she shows up and wants to help me with every damned thing a man does. I'm surprised she doesn't offer to wipe my butt."

Her neighbor's statement caught her by surprise. "Earl, that's a terrible thing to say."

"It's the truth. The woman's a pest and I want her to go away."

"Okay, at the end of the week, if you're better we'll relieve her of her duties."

"Good, I don't think my stomach can take anymore."

Cora patted him on the arm. "You and your stomach. You don't miss many meals."

"A man's got to survive, don't he?"

"I think she means more to you than you're willing to admit."

Earl slammed his fist on the table. "Ain't no such thing."

"I think you're sweet on her."

"You're out of your mind."

Earl took a sip of his coffee and looked around. "No pie?"

"There is some cake left that Meredith brought over."

Shaking his head, Earl shouted, "Hell no! I'd rather eat a dead rat."

"How about some of Maggie's brownies?"

Her neighbor smiled and smacked his lips. "That's a lot better."

Happy to share her good news, Cora said, "JJ came by and they've reinstated my license. I'm a doctor again."

"I heard and I'm mighty proud of you. This town has come to learn that you're a lot better person than most of them." Earl took a bite of brownie. "You could've turned your back on this place and no one would've blamed you, but you didn't."

"My instinct is to help people. Of course I'd stay and do everything I could. I just wish we'd been able to help more people."

"It's a horrible thing, but it's over now and we need to be grateful."

"Earl, how come you have so much power around here? I mean, you led the way to get my license back and I'd like to know what you've done in the past that gives you that much persuasive power over people."

Earl looked away. "I didn't do anything."

"Don't tell me that. I don't believe it for one minute."

He spread out his arms. "I'm an old man. You live as long as I have you make a lot of friends and a few enemies. I'm lucky to have made mostly friends and I'm not shy about asking for favors."

"But you built a hospital."

Earl shrugged. "The town needed one."

"Where'd you get the money?"

"My family owned a lot of land. My daddy was a tax man and during the dust bowl he bought up a lot of land and kept it. Later it became worth a small fortune. Same with Arthur and Big Jim Dixon."

"So you three were friends?"

"Best of pals. I miss Big Jim to this day. Nothing I wouldn't do for his daughter, Caroline, and Arthur is a man the whole town can trust and depend on."

Reaching over, Cora touched Earl's clean-shaven face and smiled. "I think you're wonderful."

"That depends." He laughed. "Just ask Meredith."

"You and her are never going to be friends, are you?"

"Nope and the same goes with Winters. Soon as possible I want her out of my house."

"Don't cut off your nose to spite your face. She's quite fond of you."

He angled his chin. "How do you know that?"

Teasing, Cora smiled. "A woman can tell."

"I don't believe you."

"You mean you've never noticed how she fusses about the house, cooking dinner, and how she wears a nice dress with her hair fixed every day?"

"That don't' mean nothing."

Cora propped her chin on her hand and stared at Earl. "That's a woman in love."

CHAPTER SEVEN

Virgil received a call from the judge and hurried over to the courthouse for the meeting he'd requested. Inside the chamber, the District Attorney, John Osborn, relaxed in front of the judge's desk smoking a cigarette.

Virgil shook hands and pulled up the other seat. "What's up, gentlemen?"

"We've just decided to launch a preliminary investigation into the operations taking place in the Missouri State Penitentiary for Women."

"Cora's not going to like that."

Osborn leaned forward, bracing his elbows on his knees. "I can't imagine she will, but she'll be called to testify even if it's not what she wants. We need evidence and she has it. We also have an inside source who can confirm everything she says."

The judge puffed on his pipe. "I tried to avoid calling Cora and leave her out of this, but to win, we can't. We want to change things that we know are going on behind those walls. She has to think of those less fortunate who are left behind."

"I think it's fear and she's scared of what they'll do to her. I don't blame her. Remember, Ted Young was murdered and, if I was to guess, I'd say the warden's behind the whole mess." Virgil rubbed his hands together. "And after meeting Judge Martin, I know the man is capable of anything under the sun to save his son's ass and maintain his good name."

Osborn looked at him. "Do you think his son, Daniel Martin, killed Cora's sister?"

"Yes. I don't know the motive and I can't prove anything, but according to the ME, Beck, he claims Eleanor was murdered and Judge Martin changed the cause of death on the official papers."

"We've learned a few things and we're going after Warden Becker on criminal charges. Not only have they been treating those women like animals, they've been making a profit off of them as well."

Virgil wrinkled his brow. "How?"

"Prostitution at the very least. Perhaps other things. We have to shut that place down. However, no one in St. Louis wants that."

"How can we prove all this?"

"We're setting up an inquest. We'll question people there and those who've been there."

"I know Cora has done everything in her power to keep me from finding out the truth about her past. With prostitution on the table, I understand why."

"I've submitted the necessary papers and I'm confident the Attorney General will give us the go ahead to have a hearing." Osborn looked at Virgil. "I'm sorry but I'll be sending Cora a subpoena and she'll have to appear. I'm leaving it up to you to see she's there."

Garner straightened. "What judge do we have?"

"Jacob Steinberg. He's fair and he's good."

Judge Garner looked at Virgil. "I'll try to smooth the way for Cora."

The District Attorney left and Virgil looked at the judge. "I should've known all along. She was so scared, so mistrusting."

"Virgil, you have to realize we've just scratched the surface. There is much more to come. Things you don't want to hear."

"I know. I know, but if it will take her pain away, I don't care. I can take it. I just hope she can."

"Cora's strong and she knows what's right. Let's just hope that in the end, Becker goes down."

"I'd like to see them all go straight to hell."

"If Eleanor's death has anything to do with what's going on in the prison, we might get our chance. That happens, they can all pay the price."

"I still need to know what they're up to. Sure, there's a little money is prostitution, and stuff like that, but Martin, Becker and Williams are into something bigger. Badder."

The judge leaned back. "I still have Batcher checking out as much as he can. I don't' want to push too hard because he's in a very dangerous situation up there."

"I know and it's troubling. I just want it all out in the open and over with."

"I hope Cora agrees with you."

Virgil left the judge's chambers and headed for Cora's. As he entered the living room, she and Dr. Lowery sat on the couch.

"Hello, Sheriff. I was just going over Cora's new duties as a doctor at General Hospital. We're awfully proud to have her."

He shook hands with the doctor and grinned. "You should be."

The doctor left and excitement oozed from her body. Her pretty face glowed with renewed hope. A big smile charmed her face. He decided tonight wasn't the time to bring up the conversation that took place in the judge's office.

But when he looked at her he couldn't help but wonder how she'd survived so much and still remained a decent person with no bitterness toward anyone. God knows, they put her through hell and yet here she stood with a smile on her face and love in her heart.

Not one of them was good enough to stand in her shadow. She was the best person he knew. The other men she'd been forced to be with didn't bother him at all. He knew in his soul, she belonged to him.

"I'm picking up Carl and Buford tonight and taking them to my dad's. We're going to talk business."

"Do you think your father is open to helping them out?"

"I'm not sure. They need some cash to get the whole thing off the ground, but maybe Briggs can help with that."

"Good luck. I'm going to get caught up on housework because tomorrow I report to the hospital."

He hugged her. "I'm so proud of you."

"I know and I can't tell you how excited I am." Holding out her hand, she said, "Look at how I'm shaking."

"You'll do just fine."

"I hope so."

Virgil and his two friends arrived at his dad's house, just as his mother had put out cookies and coffee.

"Dad, I wanted Buford and Carl to hear what you have to say about running a filling station and get an estimate on the money they'd need."

"Well, the big thing is to fill the gas tanks in the ground. They're completely empty and it cost about a hundred dollars for that. Then you've got to get the power turned on, and pay the taxes for next year."

Carl brushed his hair off his forehead. "I don't know where we can get a cent. Money is so tight."

Buford looked around. "I appreciate you all bringing me in on this, but I ain't got no money to put into this deal. I live from paycheck to paycheck."

Virgil wasn't going to let the opportunity slip through their fingers without trying every angle they could think of first.

"How much are the taxes, Dad?"

"Seventy-five dollars."

"Okay, so one hundred and seventy-five dollars will open the doors?"

"Not exactly." His father scratched his head. "You'll need supplies, son. Tires, motor oil, tools for Carl and Buford to work on cars, grease, and uniforms. Not to mention snacks, soda pop and things like that. People don't just come to a gas station for gas these days."

"How much do you think we'd need for all that?"

"Maybe close to five hundred dollars."

Carl whistled. "That a lot of moola."

Virgil's father took a sip of coffee. "I can chip in a little and help until you get started. Once you're up and running you'll have to pay me back. But, you'll still need about two hundred more dollars."

Virgil set down his cup of coffee. "I think I might be able to help with that. And the rest we'll ask Briggs."

"You thinking of selling your land, Virgil," Carl asked.

"It's just sitting there. I'd consider it an investment. You'd pay me back with interest."

"But what if we don't make it," Buford asked. "I mean, this is a tough business and we have a big, fancy place right across the street."

Carl leaned back. "That's right."

Virgil's father hooked his arm over the back of the chair. "I gave that business up because I was afraid of a little competition and I regret that." He looked at his wife. "Minnie wanted to retire and I sort of went along with that idea because I didn't want people in this town to think I'd failed."

"You didn't," Carl said. "You retired."

"I *retired* because I was afraid Eddie and Son's would run me out of business and I'd look the fool."

Buford shook his head. "I don't think that would've happened. People liked going to your filling station. You were always fair."

"I made a mistake. I should've held out at least long enough to see what would've happened. That's why I've never considered selling the place until now."

Virgil put his hand on his father's arm. "Dad, I think these men, with your help, can make that business successful again."

"I hope you're right." Virgil's father looked at Carl then Buford. "Okay, I'll take a chance on you, but, you're going to have to be willing to put in a lot of hours. And understand it's going to be awhile before you have any real money in your pocket."

"I'm preparing for that," Buford said. "I told Nell she can't quit her job."

"Okay, let's get this all on paper and meet with Briggs. Also you have to come up with a way to pay me and my father back."

Carl leaned forward. "Why are you doing this?"

"I want you to have a break." Virgil cleared his throat. "Buford, you're being used by the gas station. They're not paying you half of what you're worth."

"I know that."

"Then it's settled, we're in business."

"Let me warn you. The place will need cleaning up. I haven't stepped inside for months."

Virgil chuckled. "That's the least of our worries."

CHAPTER EIGHT

The next morning, Cora was so nervous about her first day at work that her hands wouldn't work properly as she slipped the dress over her head. Maggie was taking Jack and Tommy to school and Virgil had to be at the office early. This gave her a little time to settle down and enjoy an extra cup of coffee before she had to leave.

Excited, she bundled up in her coat and walked toward the hospital which was on the other side of town, closer to the mines and other industries.

When she arrived at the impressive, white stone building, she stopped and took a deep breath. This was a new beginning for her and she planned to do her best to serve the community. She whispered a silent prayer, straightened her shoulders and smiled. She could do this.

Inside, she found Dr. Lowery waiting for her. "Good morning, Cora. I know you're not familiar with the hospital so I thought I'd be your guide today."

She looked around and smiled. "Wonderful, since I'm lost already."

"You won't be for long. The three floors are set up identically. The nurse's stations are in the same locations, operating rooms on all three floors, and rooms have the same numerical order." He introduced her to several other personnel as they passed. "You know the emergency room is on the bottom floor. That's the only difference."

"I am familiar with that area."

On the second floor, he opened a small office that had her nameplate on the outside of the door. "This is your office."

It was half the size her office in St. Louis had been, but she didn't mind at all. She removed her coat and hung it on the tree stand just inside the door. "I love it."

"Good." He turned and walked out, motioning her to follow. "We're having an informal staff meeting so you can get acquainted with the other doctors and nurses."

They entered a room and several people sat around the table drinking coffee and talking hospital chatter. She noticed Dr. Adams who'd been so incompetent in the emergency room sitting next to Nurse Hill, who'd also given her a hard time. They both had their arms crossed, their eyes narrowed.

They weren't glad to see her.

Also, Dr. Janson, the director over the doctors was there, and he obviously didn't like her being there, either. She thought less of him because during the epidemic he'd come up with a convenient excuse to be out of town.

However, Senior Nurse Jackson was very pleasant and seemed happy to see her, the same for Dr. Westley. She also met Dr. John Early and Dr. Jeffery Ogden, who acted genuinely happy to welcome her on staff.

"When are we replacing Elbert Levy as Hospital Administrator?" Dr. Janson asked, his tiny, brown eyes glaring at her with open hostility.

"That's up to Earl Clevenger and Arthur Bridges," Dr. Lowery replied. "They'll keep us apprised of their decision."

"Don't you think we should have a say in the matter?"

"Let's let things settle down a little before we worry about something that can wait." Dr. Lowery held out his hand to her. "Shall we go? I have several things to go over with you before your shift ends."

As they exited the door, Dr. Janson called out. "Dr. Williams, be sure to drop by my office before you leave this evening."

Cora shared a cautious glance at Dr. Lowery. "He might not like the idea that you're here, but there's nothing he can do to stop it. I suggest you just stay out of his way. He's a very bitter man."

"Why?"

"Very nasty situation happened several years ago. Rumor has it he was having an affair with a nurse, his wife found out and came after him with a gun. During the struggle he shot and killed her."

"Did he go to prison?"

"He wasn't even arrested. The entire thing was dismissed as an unfortunate accident. We never mention it."

She smiled. "Nothing like hospital gossip."

"Oh, there's always that."

They had lunch in a small cafeteria in the basement of the hospital and true to form, the food was horrible. She'd be carrying her lunch from now on.

Afterwards, Dr. Lowery explained her area of the hospital. She'd be responsible for patients who were admitted to the hospital without being sent by their regular physician. That was the way most hospitals operated. She would be on the second floor. Excited, she made time to go into each room and introduce herself to her new patients.

She was happy to go back to her office for a few minutes and try to absorb all she'd learned. It was going to be tough getting back into the routine of everything, but she knew she could do it because that was what she wanted.

When Dr. Lowery told her the salary she'd be earning, Cora nearly gasped. She and Jack could afford more things for the house and better clothing. When she realized she could eventually buy a new house, the idea didn't appeal to her. No matter what, she'd stay in Aunt Rose's house because that was home for her and Jack.

She made an effort to go down to visit Nurse Hill to explain that she wanted them to get along and let the past go. She had no idea if that meant anything to the aging woman. Her skeptical expression didn't bode well. Without commenting, Nurse Hill turned and walked away.

Reluctantly, she stopped by Dr. Janson's office. He sat behind a desk twice the size of hers, flipping through several files.

"You wanted to see me before I left?"

"Yes, close the door and take a seat."

Cora carefully eyed the physician before complying.

After several minutes he looked up at her and tossed the folders on his desk. "I'll come right out and say it. I don't want you here. I don't think you're worth a damn as a doctor and I will do nothing to encourage you to stay."

Cora blinked then leaned back in the chair. She was a woman in a man's profession, Dr. Janson wasn't her first critic and she doubted he'd be the last.

"That's unfortunate, Dr. Janson. I was hoping we could work well together as professionals. Now I see you aren't a professional or even polite. Don't think you can scare me, threaten me, or push me around. Others better than you have tried and failed." She stood. "I'm here to stay. The question you should concern yourself with is, are you?"

She turned and left his office, slamming the door in her wake. A tiny smile hovered around her lips. The man had actually sputtered.

Heading for home, she pulled her coat tighter and enjoyed the feel of the cold air against her cheeks. Dr. Lowery drove by and offered her a ride, but she declined, wanting to enjoy the walk. Being in prison made her appreciate the freedom of walking down a street freely.

It dawned on her that she could probably afford a car if she wanted one, but that didn't seem important right now. Instead, she only thought about being able to buy Jack that bat he'd been looking at in the store window for the last two months. Soon it would be spring and time for sports. He wanted to play baseball.

Life was good and Cora felt like the luckiest woman alive. There was nothing more she could ask for. She had everything and so much more. As she neared home, she saw Miss Winters and Earl strolling toward her. Waving at them, she met them at the gate. "Aren't you two freezing?"

Miss Winters, with her reddened cheeks smiled. "We're enjoying a little fresh air." She looped her arm through Earl's. "Besides, this one spends too much time sitting in a chair. His legs can use the exercise."

"I'll have you know my legs are just fine."

Miss Winters smiled up at him. "I'm sure they are."

Cora shook her head and stepped past the couple to the front door of her home. Jack and Pal greeted her enthusiastically at the door. "How'd you like being a doctor again?" Jack asked. "Did you cut someone open?"

"No, far too calm of a day for that." She ruffled his hair. "How was school?"

"Good. Miss Jones brought cupcakes because it was Susie's birthday."

"Oh, that's always good news."

"What's for supper, I'm hungry?"

"When aren't you hungry?"

Jack shrugged and darted into his room with Pal racing behind him. He hadn't changed from his school clothes yet and she hoped she didn't have to continue harping at him.

Cora removed her coat and went to the kitchen. She'd set out a chicken to fry for dinner tonight and as she leaned down to take several potatoes out of the bin in the cabinet, she noticed they were running low on groceries.

As she cleaned the vegetables, the idea that she automatically assumed Virgil would be there for dinner and planned to make biscuits startled her. Since when was Virgil sharing her home being taken for granted? Yes he'd been there to protect her, but lately nothing had happened to make them think her life was in jeopardy.

Strange how easily they turned her home into *their* home. Also, the assumption that Virgil would always be a part of their family when she knew that could very well not be the case.

Just as she finished dusting the chicken with flour, salt and pepper, Earl and Miss Winters came in the back door.

"Whatcha cooking?" her neighborhood asked, rubbing his belly. "Smells good."

"Nothing is cooking, yet." Cora wiped her hands on the apron she wore and hugged Miss Winters. "How is our patient doing?"

The part-time nurse smiled, making her wrinkled face look years younger. Staring up at him, she patted him on the chest. "The walk did him a world of good. He's doing wonderfully."

"Course I am. You two make too much of nothing. I'm able to care for myself and I'll be glad when all this fussing stops."

"Oh, I don't think you honestly want us to quit, Earl," Cora teased. "You're getting used to being fretted over."

"That's not true," he said, shaking his head. "I'm getting darned annoyed, that's all."

"Today we went to visit some friends we hadn't seen in years," Miss Winters said. "Funny how you can live in such a small town and go so long without visiting people you've known all your life."

Cora turned back to the stove. "I guess that's true. Have you two had dinner?"

"Yes," Miss Winters answered quickly.

Looking over her shoulder, Cora captured the sour expression on Earl's face. He still didn't like her cooking.

"You having any dessert?"

"Now, Earl, you're to stay away from all that sugar. Doctor's orders."

"I can have a piece of pie if I want it."

"Not today." She took his arm and practically dragged him out of the house. "We're trying to get you feeling better."

The door shut behind a grumbling Earl and Cora laughed out loud. Maybe Earl wasn't so sold on this new romance.

CHAPTER NINE

Virgil practically ran upon Cora's porch and opened the door. The rich aroma of chicken frying tickled his nose. If his guess was right there would be fresh biscuits to go along with the meal.

"Hi, everyone," he called. Pal ran in circles, barking while Jack hugged his legs.

"Hi, Uncle Virgil. Did you shoot anyone today?"

"Nope, not today."

"Looks like I had the most exciting day."

"How'd you do that?" Virgil bent down and shook his finger. "Did you pay Sally a nickel for a kiss?"

"No, the next best thing." Jack grinned with excitement. "We had cupcakes."

"Oh, that does make for a good day. You're a lucky boy."

"Aunt Cora didn't cut anyone open today, either."

Virgil shook his head. "It sure gets boring around here sometimes."

"You're telling me."

Tossing off his hat and jacket, he followed his nose to the kitchen to find Cora at the stove cooking. Wrapping his arms around her waist, he bent down and kissed her on the cheek. "Did your first day go okay?"

"Yes, I'd say that. Some liked me and were glad I was there. Others will take a little more convincing."

"No problem. You'll eventually win them all over."

"Let's hope so."

"I see you're fixing my favorite dinner."

She gently shoved out of his embrace. "No matter what I fix it's your favorite."

"No, I like all your food, but fried chicken is at the top of the list."

"Then you're in luck tonight. And I know you'll be surprised to learn we're having biscuits."

"This is my lucky day."

While she finished cooking dinner, Virgil washed his hands and set the table. Just as they pulled out their chairs to sit, Maggie burst through the back door. "Come quick, Ervin Butcher's been shot."

Virgil grabbed his gun from the top of the icebox then slipped on his shoulder holster. As they neared the Butcher house two blocks away, Virgil ordered Maggie to stay back because he didn't know what he would be facing.

"How'd you find out about the shooting?"

Panting heavily, Maggie said between gasps for air, "My oldest, Eddie, came running into the house ninety miles an hour and said Ida shot her husband." Maggie bent over and put her hands on her knees. "I walked down to the end of the block to see if I could make out anything. That's when I saw Ervin sprawled out in the middle of the road. Ida stood over the body pulling the trigger."

Holding out his hand, Virgil said, "Okay, you stay here and let me take care of this." He drew closer to the ramshackle, tarpapered house with the crooked stove pipe on the tattered roof. Virgil pulled his gun. "Ida, you in there?"

"I'm here, Sheriff."

"You come out, you hear? And I want your hands in the air when you do."

He hadn't seen Ida Butcher in months. She rarely left the house and didn't appear the social type. If she had a friend, nobody knew about it. The only people Virgil had ever seen Ida with were her two daughters and Ervin.

Skinny as a scarecrow, she timidly stepped out the haphazard door and stopped on the porch. She didn't look like a murderer. Instead she looked downright pathetic.

She was wearing a dress that was too big and in serious need of repair. She had on no shoes even in this weather and her brown hair was long and stringy. Clearly, Ida hadn't had an easy life.

"I killed him," she said clearly. "I shot him dead."

Virgil slowly came closer as the sirens screamed in the distance. He waited for Ethan to arrive in the cruiser before he leaned over to look at Butcher's dead body. Virgil turned him over and found Ervin had been shot in the gut then several times in the back.

"What happened here, Virgil?" Ethan asked. He held his gun on Ida.

Shaking his head, Virgil said, "Let's find out."

By now Ida's two children were hanging on to her, crying their eyes out. "Maggie Cox said you shot Ervin."

"I did, she ain't lying." Ida clutched her girls, shivering.

"Why'd you do that?"

Blinking, Ida shrugged. "I guess I just got tired of me and the kids being beat on. Going hungry and half the time locked out of the house in the cold and having to sleep in the shed."

"If you were having troubles, Ida, why didn't you come to me?"

"I filled out a report with John a couple of months ago. He came out and talked to my husband, but after he left I got the worst beating I'd ever had. Couldn't get up off the floor for two days and only after Ervin left and the girls were able to help me."

"Now you've killed him."

"I know that ain't right. But he deserved it and I'd do it again."

"What about your children, Ida? What's going to become of them?"

"They'll finally have a good home with my folks in Joplin." She looked up at Virgil. "My husband never let us go visit my mom and dad. They never got to see the kids 'cause Ervin wouldn't let them. Now that he's dead everything will be better."

"Ida, I hate to arrest a woman for shooting a no account man. I wished you hadn't done it."

"I didn't have no choice, Virgil." She stepped closer so Ethan couldn't hear. "Ervin was looking at Marigold. His eyes followed her all around the house. I knew what he was thinking and I couldn't let him hurt my child."

"You think he intended to harm her?"

"I know he would've. Two years ago he did something nasty with the older Metzger girl. I told her parents but they didn't want to believe me." She looked at her bare feet. "So I just shut up and didn't say any more."

"You should've told me, Ida."

"You were still fighting the war. But I figured if her own parents wouldn't believe me why would anyone else."

"The law would have made a difference and you wouldn't be in the mess you're in now."

She glanced at the body of her dead husband. "I can't say why I did that, but I had just had too much, Sheriff. Me and my kids couldn't take anymore."

"You might go to prison."

She looked into the distance. "I've been in prison for ten years. Least now, maybe I'll be fed every day."

"I'm sorry about this."

"I don't blame you, Virgil. You're a good man, but it's hard for the law to come between a man and a wife."

"I would've in a minute. I'd have done all in my power to protect you and the girls."

"I threatened once to go tell you." She looked at him and tried to smile. "You know what he said?"

Virgil shook his head.

"Said he'd shoot you in the back when you least expected it."

Maggie took the two young girls in for the night and Ethan took Ida to jail. Tomorrow Virgil would talk to the judge and learn where he wanted to go from there.

Covering Butcher's body with a worn sheet, Virgil told a neighbor to call the undertaker so he could remove the body. There wouldn't be much of an investigation since Ida confessed to the murder. In Virgil's mind she had every right in the world to kill the bastard. What man treated his family so poorly?

On the way back to Cora's, Virgil bit back the anger that crawled up his spine and squeezed the back of his neck. Why didn't Ida come to him? How he wished she'd chosen something different. If only she'd have trusted him.

Sad and disheartened, Virgil opened the door to find Cora and Jack standing close together, wide-eyed and scared. He forced a weak grin. "It's okay. Everything is settled for the night."

With that, Cora went into the next room to get Jack ready for bed while he sat down to the meal Cora had kept warm in the oven. But he had no appetite for his favorite meal. Instead, his stomach churned.

Pushing the plate aside he picked up his coffee cup and took a sip. Cora walked over to him and he reached out and pulled her close. He buried his face in the front of her dress. "It was terrible."

Tenderly, she ran her fingers through his hair, relaxing him instantly. "Did she really kill her husband?"

He looked up at her. "Yes, but he was a beast to her and her children. She wasn't even crying."

"I hate hearing that. The poor woman. Now she'll spend her life in prison. I feel sorry for all she's been through."

"I wish I'd known."

"You can't blame yourself, Virgil."

"I just hope the judge and JJ can come up with some way to help her and her children. She doesn't belong in jail and her little girls need a mother."

"In this world we don't always get what we need, only what's given us."

"I don't know why a man would be so mean to someone he loved."

"Those kinds of men don't love. They just want to control and punish."

"Still, I can't even imagine hurting you or Jack. Just the thought makes me sick to my stomach."

She put her palms on the sides of his face. "That's because you're a good man."

"I hope I never turn into a man like Ervin Butcher."

"What about Ida? Will she be locked in jail?"

"Yes. I'll see what the judge wants to do, but she deserves better."

"What about his folks? Will Butcher's family demand she be arrested?"

Virgil rubbed his chin. "I don't know. His mother is dead and has been for years, I'm not sure about his daddy or any siblings."

"Do his relatives live here in Gibbs City?"

"Yeah, I think they do. I'll notify them tomorrow."

"I saw Maggie took her little girls. The youngest is in Jack's class." She took the plate and scraped the remains in the trash. "I'm sure she's upset that her father is dead. Worse, murdered in front of her."

"I'll talk to them." He filled his cup. "Ida told me Butcher had been eyeballing the older girl and she was afraid he might sexually molest her."

"His own child? Oh, how horrible. I'm glad she shot him."

"Yeah, let's hope others take it that way."

"I'm sorry you're caught in the middle of all this. Being sheriff is a tough job."

"I just wish she'd come to me before taking matters into her own hands. Then we wouldn't be dealing with a young woman going to prison and two girls losing both parents."

"I know, but at least now she's not suffering anymore."

He looked at Cora, his heart shuddering. "That's exactly what she said."

CHAPTER TEN

The next day, Cora stopped by the dry cleaners to let them all know she was okay in her new job and that she would miss them so much. Arthur and Helen were talking in his office. He wanted her to stay home longer to get over the death of Don, her husband. But, Helen insisted she wanted to be at work.

After Helen returned to the work area, Cora approached Arthur. "It's probably best she's working, you know. At home, she's alone and there's no one to talk to. Here, she's busy and distracted by her job, and more importantly, she's among friends."

Arthur stared down at his shoes. "I just hate to see her hurting like this."

"Give her time. It's only been a week. She needs to get her feet under her and then she'll be fine. She's a good woman. Give her time to work this out."

"Yes, she is a good person." He put his hands in his pockets and looked at Cora. "I'll keep an eye on her and let her do whatever feels right."

Cora went to work and relished in the joy of walking into the hospital and going up to her office. By the time she got there she was practically giddy. Slipping on the white lab coat, she went to the nurse's station to start her morning rounds. She knew a few of the patients and the she quickly became acquainted with the others.

A little later in the morning, she was summoned to the emergency room where she found one of Jack's young schoolmates. He'd fallen and gotten hurt at school. "My, young man, you took a serious fall."

Eyes filled with tears, he said, "I got pushed down."

"I'm sorry about that, but I think your leg is broken."

"Broken? It's really broke?" He smiled, scrubbing away the tears. "Do I get one of those casts on my leg?"

His mother looked worried to death and the kid was ready to jump up and dance at the prospect of having a cast. Something none of the other children had. Imagine the prestige.

"You won't think it's wonderful in a few weeks when it starts itching."

"Is he going to be okay?" his mother asked.

"Yes, it'll just take time to heal that's all."

"Well, that's good news. I'm not going to like having him underfoot all that time, but I glad he wasn't seriously hurt."

Cora tried to put the mother's mind at rest. "Kids, especially boys, are the worst at getting hurt. They're rough and out to conquer the world."

"I know exactly what you mean." She pushed back her son's hair lovingly. "He's the youngest of seven brothers."

"I don't envy you."

But in a way Cora did. She'd always wanted a big family with children running all around. Too bad that would never happen.

Dr. Lowery came in after the boy had been patched up and sent on his way. As she and the doctor walked the corridor, he explained he had a patient he wanted to consult with her on. He'd not been able to determine exactly what was wrong with the elderly woman.

They decided to run several tests and if they didn't find anything they'd do exploratory surgery to see what caused her pain.

CHAPTER ELEVEN

Arriving at the office, Virgil found that Ethan had already gotten Ida Butcher a plate of food and coffee from Betty's Diner.

"She told me that she hadn't eaten in two days, so I went over early this morning and got her breakfast."

"That's good."

"Never met anyone more grateful for food."

"I imagine she's had it pretty rough for a long time."

"Yeah, she didn't have any shoes. I asked her if I could go get them and she said there weren't any. She and the oldest girl shared a pair. Said Marigold needed them more."

"That's sad."

"That's downright heartbreaking."

"I'm going to see the judge. It's up to him what we do about all this."

"I hope they pin a medal on her."

Virgil knew that wasn't going to happen, but the judge was the most reasonable man he knew. After waiting several minutes for a visitor to leave, Virgil was escorted into the chamber.

"I heard Ida murdered her husband last night."

"Yes, sir."

"What are we becoming? The crime capital of the world? I'm wondering when organized gangs are going to move in."

Virgil removed his hat. "Please don't ask for any more trouble."

The judge leaned back and threaded his fingers together across his stomach. "Tell me what happened."

"It's pretty open and shut. Ida Butcher shot and killed Ervin Butcher in the middle of Liberty Street last night around five o'clock."

"She tell you why?"

"Says he was mean to her and the girls and she feared he'd developed a sexual interest in his oldest daughter."

"Hell, I'd shoot him for that myself."

"I don't honestly think Ida Butcher deserves to be in jail. I went by that house this morning and I couldn't find enough food to feed a cat, much less a family of four."

"Butcher didn't look deprived to me."

"No, but his family did."

The judge shook his head. "Ida should've never married that no good loafer."

"Did you know her?"

"Yeah, her family lived across the street from us for years. Her father is a damned good man."

Virgil leaned back in his chair. "So, why'd she marry Butcher?"

"Probably because the right man never asked her." Judge Garner cleared his throat. "I need to talk to JJ and see if we can figure a way to keep her out of prison."

"Could be that Butcher came after her and she shot him in self-defense?"

"Maybe, but she'd have to say that in a court of law and Ida's not a liar. I think it's more of a case where she got sick and tired of being shoved around and bullied."

Virgil shook his head. "I don't think that will keep her out of jail. The jury will say she should've walked away."

"That would've been the right thing to do."

Virgil sat up. "Do you think she was in her right mind?"

The judge laughed. "She might look pretty ragged right now, but she's as sharp as a tack. The smartest gal in school. There was talk of her even going to college."

"So we can't use insanity."

The judge took out his pipe and tapped the head full of sweet smelling tobacco. "We're going to have to come up with something. The County Commissioner is going to want something."

"Maybe JJ'll come up with something." Virgil looked away. "Can I at least let her get a bath, clean clothes and I'll buy her a pair of shoes."

"Go ahead. Maybe Cora will help. And I'll see the county pays for everything."

"Okay, it won't be hard to get Cora's help. What about the girls? They don't look much better."

"The law says if she has to go to court we have to make sure she looks presentable. Doesn't say anything about her children, so I'll take care of that."

Virgil left feeling that half the world leaned on him. How in the hell did all this happen in his small county?

His day didn't seem to be getting any easier. Buford, Carl and a puzzled looking Briggs waited for him. He grabbed a cup of bad coffee and quickly marched everyone into his office and closed the door. "Have a seat, fellas. I know Briggs doesn't have much time."

"What's this all about?" Briggs asked.

"We need your advice on a business deal."

Briggs nodded and took a seat. "I'll help all I can."

Virgil leaned back. "Well. First we need money."

Briggs paled. "Oh, how much?"

"Carl and Buford are thinking of buying my dad's old filling station on Main Street and they need financing."

Briggs looked at Buford and Carl. "Do you men have any money at all?"

"Only the two hundred dollars I'm loaning them," Virgil said. "And what my dad's pitching in."

"That's not much for a business. You don't have any reserve for when business is down."

"No they don't," Virgil said. "But they're both hard workers."

Briggs frowned. "Pardon my bluntness, but not Carl."

Carl put his hand on his hip. "I'm going to be a hard worker when I get a job." Briggs didn't' look convinced.

"My dad's going to help them and he has years of business experience. He'll be giving them advice."

"That's good, but still." Briggs pinched the bridge of his nose. "I don't know that the bank can stick its neck out that far."

Carl stepped forward. "Then what the hell good is the bank if they aren't willing to loan money?"

"They loan money to reliable sources."

"Humph! Reliable sources don't need to borrow money."

Buford stood leaning against the wall. "So what can we do?"

Briggs thought for a few moments then he smiled. "Have you thought of getting a business loan under the GI bill?"

Virgil propped his elbows on his desk. "Can they do that?"

"Yes, under certain circumstances. We'd have to go with Carl here because he has the service time, but let me check it out and see if I can't figure a way to apply for a GI loan."

That was a weight off Virgil's shoulders. Maybe his friends had a shot at this after all.

Carl grinned. "I didn't know we could borrow money from the government."

"Read the GI Bill. You can get a low interest loan on your house and even go to college." Briggs picked up his satchel and stood. "There's a lot of paperwork and it takes time, but I think we can pull this off."

Virgil leaned across his desk and shook Briggs' hand. "Well I'll be damned."

CHAPTER TWELVE

Cora was surprised when she came home from work and found Virgil standing in the middle of her living room with a strange woman.

He appeared uncomfortable and it seemed he wasn't sure what to do. The woman next to him was in her early forties clutching a paper sack. She looked tired and as confused as Virgil. Cora removed her coat and looked inquiringly at the two. What was going on?

Virgil took off his hat. "I'm sorry to spring this on you, but I need your help."

She stepped forward. "What can I do?"

"This is Ida Butcher. She, ah, she..."

Ida's trembled into a shy smile. "I need a bath."

Cora patted her on the shoulder and pointed her in the direction of the bathroom. "I understand completely."

"Maggie has the two girls and when they left for school, she ran to town and bought some clothes, but I brought Ida here because Maggie's house was already crowded."

"Okay, well welcome, Ida," Cora said. "Come this way to the bathroom."

Ida stopped and looked at Virgil. "Thank you for all you've done." Hugging the sack a little closer, she spoke quietly,

"I really appreciate it and so do my girls." She turned and took Cora's hand. "I'm so sorry to inconvenience you."

"No bother at all," Cora said. "I've been in a few scrapes myself."

Cora turned the light on and began running bathwater. Looking at that small bottle of lavender oil, she smiled. If anyone ever needed something extra it was Ida Butcher. Pouring in a few drops, she tossed in a handful of bubble bath and took out two clean towels.

Stepping back into the living room, Cora extended her hand to Ida and led her into the bathroom. "You can set your clothes on the vanity. Take all the time you need. There's shampoo there on the side of the tub. There's no hurry."

Ida's eyes widened at the bubbles then she sniffed. "That's lovely. I can't thank you enough."

Cora backed out and closed the door. She looked at Virgil still standing in the middle of the living room floor.

"What exactly is going on? And where is Jack?"

Virgil held up his hands. "He's across the street with Maggie, who's fixing dinner. I didn't want Ida talking a bath while she was alone in the house with me and I couldn't let her leave because she's a prisoner."

"That poor woman," Cora mused, heading for the kitchen. "We'll let her soak as long as she wants. I doubt she's had a decent bath in months. And I won't begrudge her a thing."

Maggie knocked softly and opened the door before Cora could answer. She held out a casserole wrapped in a dish towel. "I cleaned up the girls the best I could before I sent them to bed last night. When they left for school I went downtown and bought them a few dresses and some clean underwear and shoes." Placing the dish on the stove, Maggie brushed her hands on her apron. "I went to their house this morning and there wasn't anything there decent enough for a little girl to wear."

Cora hugged her friend. "I'm glad you did all that. Ida is in the tub."

"Good. I'm sure she's enjoying that, poor thing."

Cora shook her head. "It's a small thing, but you can't imagine what it meant to her after all she's been through."

Maggie turned to Virgil. "What did the judge say?"

Virgil shrugged. "Nothing yet. He and JJ are trying to figure out what to do. No one thinks she belongs in jail."

"I'll pray for her. I talked to her mother and tomorrow she's coming to get the kids."

"Can you watch them tonight?" Cora asked.

"Yes, they're fine. Well behaved young girls."

Maggie left and Cora put on a pot of coffee. Earl came in the back door madder than a caged wildcat. "What the hell happened last night?"

Virgil leaned back in his chair at the table. "Ida Butcher shot Ervin Butcher."

Earl banged his cane on the floor. "Good, the bastard deserved it."

"If you knew how bad it was there then why didn't you tell me?"

"I didn't really think it was going to come to this."

"If any woman is being mistreated, by God, I want to know about it, Earl," Virgil shouted. "It's my damned job."

Cora put her finger to her lips. "Lower your voices. Ida will hear you."

Earl shuffled over to a chair near Virgil. Sitting down, he held his cane between his knees, hands stacked on the handle. "Don't go getting all riled up. I was hoping John would take care of it."

Virgil frowned. "Well he didn't and now Ida might spend the rest of her life in the slammer."

"What did the judge say?"

"He's trying to see if he and JJ can come up with a deal."

"What kind of deal?"

"I don't know, I'm not a lawyer. And I'm not getting my hopes up. This could go either way. We could have a murder trial right here in Parker County."

Earl blinked and leaned back in the chair. "That'd be a first."

Virgil hooked his arm over the back of his chair. "And I hate that Ida has suffered so badly at the hands of that bastard. Are there any good people left in this world? I'm beginning to wonder."

"Well, we'll all stand behind her. Ain't a person in this county that will find her guilty."

"You don't know that. People are funny. And I've yet to talk to Ervin's dad. I'm going over to do that in a few minutes."

"His pappy ain't worth a damn. He's a low-down, dirty dog just like the son he raised. Lazy and mean as they come."

"He might have something to say about Ida going to prison for murdering his son."

"No, he won't."

"You don't know that, Earl."

Cora's neighbor stood. "The hell I don't."

"What are you up to now?"

Earl swung his cane, tightened his lips and lowered his brow in determination. "I'm going to keep that gal out of prison."

"Oh, God," Virgil muttered.

CHAPTER THIRTEEN

Virgil had to admit, Ida Butcher looked very nice once she had cleaned up. Her hair was long and hung straight down to the middle of her back. The dress was a size too big and he didn't think the shoes fit, but she was pretty and clean with a bright smile on her face.

"Thank you for letting me use your bathroom, Cora." She clutched her hands tightly. "And the bath was wonderful. I loved every minute."

A knock sounded at the door. He was surprised when he opened it and the judge stood outside wearing a plain shirt and trousers.

"I'm here to pick up Ida," he said with the same authority he used in his courtroom. "I'm taking her to my house for supper then I'll drop her off at the jail."

Virgil opened the door wider. "Okay, I'll call and let Ethan know."

Ida touched the judge's arm. "I'd like to go see my girls if I can, Francis."

"That's fine, Ida. But know that they're well cared for. I spoke to your mother. She's coming and will be staying at my house so the girls aren't removed from school and forced to make an unnecessary change."

Ida blushed. "That's more than kind of you, Francis."

After they left Virgil shut the door and turned a stunned look at Cora. "Did you see that?"

"I did but I'm not sure what it was I saw."

"It was the judge and Ida Butcher? Can that be possible?"

Cora shrugged. "I don't know."

"I've never heard him mention her before."

Cora moved toward the kitchen. "Maybe they knew each other when they were younger."

"But he's older than her by fifteen years."

Cora raised her hands. "Stranger things have happened."

"This has been a long, trying day and I'm dead on my feet," he admitted. "I'll go get Jack, then after supper I'm sacking out."

"Okay, but eat first."

"You're right. I didn't have supper last night because I had a murder to deal with. No wonder I'm so hungry."

"Get back here and we'll eat."

"Put the coffee on."

Playing with Tommy had worn Jack out, so Virgil carried him across the street to the back door. They woke him up so he could have supper. Helping him to the table, the boy slumped in his chair sleepily, spooning the food in his mouth. "I think Pal's tired," he mumbled.

They ate quietly, their mood subdued. Virgil reached for Jack just before he nearly fell face first into his food. Picking up the limp, little boy, Virgil put Jack to bed while Cora cleaned up. When he walked out of Jack's bedroom to the living room, Cora held out a cup of coffee. "Sit down and relax a little. You've been very busy lately."

"I meant to tell you earlier today that my dad, Buford, Carl and Briggs met at my office. They discussed buying the gas station."

"How did that go?"

He smiled. "Pretty good. Briggs thinks Carl might be able to get a loan from the government."

Cora wrinkled her brow. "Really, how?"

"Says it part of the GI bill."

"That would be wonderful." She tapped him on the chest. "But a loan means they'd still have to pay it back."

"I know, and that's the hard part. But, I'm glad Briggs is helping them."

"I honestly hope it all works out."

Virgil took a sip of coffee. "Now, I'm worried about Ida."

"I don't want to see any woman sentenced to that place. It's a hideous place that destroys your soul. People in there come out different. You're never the same again."

"I can't even imagine."

She turned to him. "I think it's safe for you to move out."

He pulled her against him and savored her warmth. "Marry me."

"I can't. Not yet."

Taking her by the shoulders he asked, "When can I make you mine?"

"There's some things I need to get past before I can make a commitment." She kissed him softly. "Know that I love you, but I'm not sure we can be together. I don't know if we'll get that chance."

"I don't care about your past."

"You don't know. There are things...things I can't talk about yet."

Virgil and Cora went to work the next day with a deep chasm between them. Virgil wanted her to forget what had happened in prison and live in the present. It angered him that she allowed the past to come between them. Did she really care for him or was this just an excuse?

CHAPTER FOURTEEN

Cora had hardly started her day and begun her rounds when she heard her name over the intercom. She returned to the nurse's station to learn that she had a phone call waiting for her.

On the other end of the line, Judge Garner's bailiff said her presence was requested in the courthouse later that morning. He had no details he was willing to share.

She didn't think she'd have a problem getting off work, but she was surprised that the judge wanted to see her. Perhaps it was about Ida Butcher, but Cora didn't know her that well and didn't feel she could add much to the case.

After leaving the hospital in the bitter cold, she quickly made her way toward the town square. From General Hospital, that was close to a fifteen minute walk. Looking up at the gray sky, she hoped it wouldn't start snowing.

She checked her timepiece as she neared the Sheriff's office. Deciding she had a few minutes to stop by and warm up and possibly learn what the judge wanted, she opened the door and stepped inside.

Virgil greeted her with a wide grin. "What are you doing here? Don't they need you at the hospital?"

Holding her hands out to accept the warmth from the potbelly stove, she said, "I'm sure they do. But Judge Garner sent word he wanted to see me."

Virgil sat up and frowned. "Really, I received the same message. I wonder what's going on."

"I was hoping you'd know more than I did."

"Sorry, no such luck. I'm assuming it has something to do with Ida, but I can't see where you getting involved can help."

Cora shivered. "That's what I thought."

"Well, it's about time we leave. Don't want to be late." He called back to Ida. "I won't be long. I left the door unlocked should you need the privy."

"I'm fine, Sheriff. My mother should be here soon."

Crossing the street, Cora saw Arthur and Ester getting out of a car. They headed for the courthouse as well. Virgil called out. "Arthur, did the judge call you?"

The pair hesitated then turned. As they drew closer, Arthur said, "Yes, his bailiff said Judge Garner wanted to see Ester and me." They approached the steps. "Do you know what it's about?"

Virgil shook his head. "No idea. But he called Cora and me as well."

"Strange, isn't it?"

The friendly man who assisted the judge showed them into the chambers. "Take a seat and the judge will be right with you."

Virgil and Arthur sat in the two chairs in front of the judge's desk while Cora and Ester sat on a small couch against the wall.

Arthur balanced his hat on his knee while Virgil leaned forward with his arms braced on his knees.

"What's taking so long?" Arthur asked. "I have to get back to the dry cleaners."

Before Virgil could answer, the door opened and Bart Cooper shoved the judge so hard, he sprawled on the floor then struggled to stand.

Pointing a gun at them, Bart smiled and gently closed them off from the rest of the world. "So glad to see you could all make it." Bart looked slightly disheveled and sweat beaded on his shiny forehead.

"Bart," Arthur shouted. "What in God's name are you up to now?"

Judge Garner staggered to his chair and slumped down. "He was waiting in my office this morning when I arrived at the courthouse. Says he's killing everyone. He made me ask Jessie, my bailiff, to call you all here."

"Does Jessie know?" Virgil asked.

"No one knows you're in here for anything but a friendly chat." Bart sneered. "I planned the whole thing and I'm going to get away with murder. See if I don't."

Virgil slowly rose from his chair, holding out his hands. "You need to put down that gun before you do something you'll regret."

"Oh, hell, I can't begin to tell you the things I regret, Sheriff." He moved the gun toward Ester who screamed and clutched Cora. "Including marrying that sniveling bitch."

Arthur angrily shoved himself up. "That's enough, Bart. I demand you put down that gun and let the ladies go."

The gun exploded and Arthur collapsed to the floor.

CHAPTER FIFTEEN

Virgil's hand reached to grab Bart's gun, but Bart was too quick. "Stand back, Sheriff, or you're next." He took Virgil's gun and held a gun in each hand.

Cora cautiously moved to attend to Arthur, while Ester sat frozen in fear, her hand clutching her chest. Quickly opening the man's clothing, Cora pulled back the shirt to reveal a hole in his shoulder. "You could've killed him. I need to call an ambulance before he bleeds to death."

"We're not doing a damned thing. Let the bastard lay there and die."

The ugly smirk on Bart's face had Virgil worried. Bart was a dangerous man right now because he didn't have anything to lose. Obviously he had no intention of going back to jail and now he was out for revenge against those he felt had done him wrong.

"Bart, it's not too late to clean this all up. You kill us in cold blood, the law will never stop looking for you. For the rest of your life, you'll be a hunted man."

"You think I care?"

"You should," the judge said. "There are a lot worse things than being arrested."

"Shut up, you old son of a bitch. You sit up here in your house of authority and divvy out justice like you're some kind of

God." Bart's face reddened. "Well, you're not. Not today. Today you're going to die."

"Bart, I don't understand any of this," Ester screamed. "I can't believe you shot my daddy."

"Shut up." Bart shook the gun, shoving it against Ester's cheek. "Shut up or I'll blow your brains out."

Virgil stepped closer. "Bart, look at me." He moved a little closer. "Let's you and me fix this."

Bart turned one of the guns on Virgil. "You shut up too, you big know-it-all. You and that bitch have done nothing but cause me trouble. Now I'm killing the whole damned lot of you." Bart cocked the guns.

Without warning, the door flew open and Carl staggered through the door. His hat was on backwards, his coat hung from one arm and he reeked of liquor.

"Hey, Virgil," Carl said as he tripped over toward him. "I come to tell you that the bank said we could have the money."

"It's old, drunk Carl," Judge Garner said. "Get out of here before you get killed."

Bart ran over and shut the door.

Carl turned around, blinked and smiled drunk as a skunk. "What's everyone doin'? Havin' a party?" He slurred his words so badly Virgil could barely understand.

Bart poked him with the gun. "Get over there in that corner and shut up."

"I come here to tell my good buddy, Virgil, the good news." Carl reached out to hug Virgil and stumbled forward, making him have to reach out and catch Carl before he hit the floor. That's when he felt Carl shove the gun into the belt at his waist.

Virgil and Carl shared a look. He wasn't drunk, it was all a trick. Carl may have saved their lives. Slowly Virgil pretended to guide his buddy to the corner of the room by the door, securing the weapon. Once there, Carl knocked on the door.

Ethan burst into the room as Virgil whipped out the gun Carl had given him. When Bart lifted the barrel of the gun toward Ethan, Virgil fired twice.

Cora and Ester screamed, but Ethan ran forward and kicked the guns away from Bart's outstretched hands. Virgil reached for a pulse and didn't feel anything. "I'm afraid he's dead."

"Good damned riddance," Judge Garner said, rubbing the back of his head. "That man was insane. He planned to kill all of us."

Ethan reached down and picked up Virgil's weapon and handed it to him then holstered his own sidearm. Looking from the body to Virgil he nodded at Carl. "He ran me down at the diner and told me he saw Bart sneaking around the courthouse with the judge. I knew that wasn't right. I checked with the bailiff and he said that all of you were inside."

Carl straightened his clothes. "That's when I remembered the threats he made to come back and kill you. Ethan and I knew one of us had to make it into the room, after all, who'd suspect a drunk charging in to save the day?"

The ambulance came and took the unconscious Arthur away. Ester followed, appearing fearful her father wouldn't make it. Cora quickly assured her that he would be fine.

Virgil reached out and shook Carl's hand. "I'm really grateful for your help."

"Wasn't anything you wouldn't do for me."

"You put your life on the line for us and you deserve a medal," the judge said.

"I don't want nothing but a decent cup of coffee and a piece of apple pie." He slapped Ethan on the shoulder and the two men headed out the door.

Cora went around and checked out the judge's head. "You took a nasty hit. I suggest you let the sheriff drive you to the hospital to be checked out."

"Naw, I'm fine."

Virgil held out his hand. "Come on, Judge. Doctor's orders. Besides, I'm heading that way to return Cora back to work."

Reluctantly he stood and they left the chamber where just moments before Virgil hadn't been sure anyone would walk out alive.

Virgil left the hospital with the knowledge that Judge Francis Garner was doing well and, after a night's rest, he'd be sent home. Arthur's injury was more serious and required surgery to remove the bullet followed by an overnight stay the hospital.

After learning her father would be fine, Ester asked for and received something for her nerves. Afterwards Virgil drove Ester home then returned to his office to fill out a mountain of paperwork.

Carl and Ethan were still patting themselves on the backs for being so clever when Virgil strode in and hugged them so tightly he thought they might not be able to breathe. Releasing his pals, he stepped back and grinned.

"You guys sure pulled a fast one."

"It was all Carl," Ethan said. "He saw Bart and knew something was up."

"I didn't do anything but give Virgil a gun. You two had all the shooting power."

"Did you guys ever get that coffee and pie?"

"We sure did and when a few people in the diner heard what happened, they offered to pay. We were sure lucky."

Virgil realized they all had been very fortunate to have walked out of there alive. He had seen in Bart's eyes that he was determined to kill all of them. Now he was the one dead, lying on a slab in the basement of the hospital.

Carl picked up his hat and headed for the door. "I've got an appointment with Briggs. He's going to help me fill out the application for the GI loan. Wish me luck."

With a new found respect, Virgil watched his friend hurry down the street. He held his head a little higher and had a bit of a swagger to his walk, but Virgil had always known the man he'd fought with in the war was somewhere inside the town drunk.

Watching Ethan hunt and peck at the Remington typewriter with the speed of a snail, Virgil asked, "How's Ida doing?"

"Her mother came by earlier and visited for a while. I overheard Ida say she was sorry she killed Butcher but she told her mother he was so mean to them she couldn't take it anymore."

"That's too bad."

"Yeah, they were back there bawling for a long time. I think they're both afraid of her going to prison."

"As of right now, no charges have been filed, so if the judge doesn't do something pretty soon we won't be able to hold her."

"Really?"

"That's the way the law reads." Virgil looked out the window and saw JJ coming toward his office. He opened the door and welcomed in the County Attorney. "Howdy, JJ. I guess you've heard?"

JJ set down his briefcase, took off his hat and unbuttoned his coat. "I've heard enough to fill a newspaper. Between Ervin Butcher and Bart Cooper, our little county is going to start making big time news reports."

"I hope not," Ethan said. "Doesn't look good having two shootings in a town this small. I like it best when the biggest trouble is a pack of dogs on the loose. I'm ready to go back to peace and quiet. And I hate filling out these endless witness reports." Jerking the form out of the typewriter, he wadded it up and threw it into the overflowing trash can.

"That's not likely to happen for some time now."

JJ thumbed to the back of the office. "How's Ida holding up?"

"Her mother was here earlier and you can imagine they're both worried sick about what is going to happen."

"Well, she'll be charged with murder. It will be up to the judge to determine if there is a trial or not."

"I think he might be toting a headache today. Bart smacked him pretty good."

JJ slapped the desk. "That man was insane. I can't believe he came back here to try to kill you guys. Only a crazy person would think they could get away with something like that."

Virgil shook his head. "We'd all probably be dead if it wasn't for Carl's quick thinking."

JJ whistled. "I heard. Thank God for that."

"Let me know what to do with Ida. If she gets formally charged I'll have to turn her over to the Carthage Police Chief."

"I plan to check with the judge later." JJ picked up his briefcase. "I have to be at the courthouse in a few minutes. I'll see you later." He pointed to Virgil. "You'll also have to do the paperwork for shooting Bart."

Ethan snickered behind him.

"I know. I'll work on that this afternoon."

CHAPTER SIXTEEN

After the exciting morning Cora had, she was grateful to be able to do her rounds and relieved that Bart would no longer be a worry. When she left for work this morning, she had no idea the day would turn out so strange.

Cora finally had a moment to go in and check on Arthur. She was surprised to find Helen sitting at his bedside. "Hello, how are you doing?"

Helen stood. "I just dropped by to see how Arthur was. We heard about the incident at the courthouse and I told the girls at the dry cleaners I'd check and see if he needed anything."

"That's very nice of you. How is everyone?"

"We're all good. You sure are missed a lot." Helen smiled. "But we keep reminding ourselves you're doing what you've always wanted to do."

"True, but I miss seeing you girls every day for our coffee breaks and the customers."

"I bet you don't miss Henry and Reverend Fuller."

"No, I don't." Cora paused. "Where is the reverend?"

Helen shrugged. "I've seen him around town a few times helping those who are still getting back on their feet after losing loved ones in the epidemic."

Arthur mumbled something then dozed back off. When Cora saw the concerned look on Helen's face, she said, "He's still groggy from surgery. They had to dig a bullet out of his shoulder, so he's heavily sedated."

"Is he going to be okay?"

"Yes, he'll have to spend some time healing, and that arm might be a little stiff for a while, but in all seriousness he's lucky Bart didn't kill him."

Helen put her hands to her chest. "My God, when we heard, we were shocked. I never in a million years expected Bart to do something that foolish." She looked away. "Now he's dead."

Cora went over and put her arm around her friend. With the recent loss of her husband, Helen had a difficult time with people dying, which was only normal. "It's okay. He was a bad man out to harm other people."

"I know, but so many have passed away." She looked at Cora. "I heard about Ida Butcher, too. I thought that woman wouldn't hurt a fly. She's one of the nicest people in this town."

"I never knew her, but it's all tragic. Especially because of the children."

"Someone said her mother was coming to care for them."

"I think that's right." Cora looked around. "Where is Arthur's daughter, Ester?"

"Her nerves were too bad. The whole episode was too hard on all of us. The nurse said they gave her something to calm her down and Virgil took her home."

"Oh, dear, I hope he wakes up before I leave for the day. I don't want him to be alone."

"He won't be," Helen said. "I'll be here until I see for myself that he's okay."

"Good," Cora said, walking out the door. "I'll check by again before I leave."

She went to the second floor and pushed into Judge Garner's room. It seemed strange to see the proper and powerful judge propped up in a hospital bed, wearing a cotton night shirt.

"Hello, Judge. How's the head."

"Hurts like the dickens. I wish Bart was alive so I could coldcock him."

"I don't think Virgil had much choice there."

"No, he didn't and I'm thankful to God he did what needed to be done. I've no doubt Bart would've stuck to his word about killing us."

"I'm afraid you're right."

The judge adjusted his pillow. "How's Arthur?"

"I just came from his room and he's still sleeping from the surgery, but expected to make a full recovery. Helen Green is sitting with him."

"Good, I thought he was a goner when Bart fired that gun. The crazy lunatic."

"Our peaceful little town isn't so peaceful lately."

"I know, I've been thinking about Ida."

Cora took his hand. "I know this is none of my business and I don't want to sway your opinion, but there are times in a woman's life when an injustice just can't continue." She squeezed. "Please try to remember that."

"I will Cora."

He looked pale. The ordeal they'd experienced had taken a toll on him and she knew it would be some time before he got over the events that happened. "You stay in bed until you're released." She pointed a finger at him. "Don't let me catch you sneaking out of the hospital."

The judge grumbled. "I can't. They took my clothes and left me wearing this." He tugged at the night shirt. "Can't get far dressed like this."

She laughed. "That's our plan."

Exhausted, Cora grabbed a cup of coffee from the nurse's station and returned to her office to read through some files. She'd just taken her first sip when Virgil knocked on her open door.

"What are you doing here?"

He leaned against the frame of the door. She didn't like the look on his face. "I've moved my things out of your house. I won't be sleeping there anymore."

Dread choked her, threatening her air supply. "I see."

"I'm not saying I won't be coming around, because I'd still like to do that, but I think we both know it's best I don't stay the night."

She licked her lips. "I think you're right."

He stepped in further and closed the door. "I want to be with you, Cora. And knowing that there is a wall separating us is driving me crazy. I don't know how long I can keep my hands to myself and I know you're not ready."

She looked into his pale blue eyes. "I want the same thing you do. I just don't want to make a mistake."

"I can't imagine us making love would ever be a mistake."

She wanted to confess every wrong she'd ever done, everything that kept her awake at night and every hope that'd been dashed behind those prison walls. But she couldn't. Not today.

"I know it's asking a lot, Virgil. But please be patient and know I love you and never want to hurt you."

"I know that and it makes me wonder why I feel so empty inside."

CHAPTER SEVENTEEN

Virgil left Cora's office with a heart that felt like a ten ton boulder was on his chest. As a peace offering, she'd invited him to dinner tonight. Neither one of them wanted him to be completely removed from Jack's life.

Before stopping at the office, he drove to Betty's Diner and bought Ida a slice of pie. He ran into Reverend Fuller having a meal with the Nelson family who'd lost all their children.

"Afternoon, Sheriff," Fuller called out. "Mr. and Mrs. Nelson and I were just talking about opening the church back up. Do you think that's possible?"

"I'm not sure. You'll have to talk to Earl and Arthur, but both are a little under the weather. Earl is still weak from the flu and Arthur was shot today in Judge Garner's chamber by Bart Cooper."

"Oh dear," Mrs. Nelson said. "Is he all right?"

"He's expected to be fine, but he needs rest. I'll get Ethan to get a few men and clean the cots and things out of the church and replace the pews."

"I'd appreciate that." Fuller put his cup down. "How is Miss Williams?"

Virgil grew cautious. "Her medical license was reissued and she's working at General Hospital."

The man who'd practically assaulted Cora, smiled. "I've been praying that God would bless her and it appears he has."

Virgil took the paper sack and left the diner. He didn't know what to think about the reverend but he knew he still didn't trust him. Not where Cora and Jack were concerned.

Back at his office, Virgil caught the aroma of freshly brewed coffee. He walked back to find Ida Butcher sitting in the corner of her cell on a small chair Ethan had provided with a cup in her hand.

"Afternoon, Sheriff. I hope you don't mind that I fixed a pot of coffee."

He didn't mind at all. With all that had happened, Virgil didn't keep Ida's cell door locked. Her two girls were in town and she wouldn't ever leave without them. "I brought you a piece of cherry pie."

She held out her hand. "You and Ethan are fattening me up like a Thanksgiving turkey. I'll be so fat I won't be able to fit through the door."

There wasn't a chance in hell that would ever happen. She was so skinny she could probably squeeze through the bars if she took a notion. "I don't think that's something we have to worry about."

Virgil handed her the pie then poured himself a cup of brew.

Ida took a bite then looked at Virgil. "How's Francis? I heard he got a nasty bump on the head."

"He's okay. They insisted he stay the night in the hospital for observation, but he should be up and around tomorrow."

"I was sure worried when I first heard. I wouldn't want anything to ever happen to him."

"Do you two know each other?"

"You could say that, but it was all a long time ago. I won't say anything else about me and Francis. The past is the past."

Virgil drove to the hospital to look in on the two patients. Helen was with Arthur who sat up drinking water through a straw. "I'm damned lucky to be alive."

"We all are," Virgil said. "Damned lucky, indeed."

"You be sure and tell Carl I appreciate what he did. Not many men would take a chance like that."

"I'll pass that along. You take care of yourself."

He left Arthur's room and journeyed downstairs to see the judge. He was sitting in bed grimly looking out the window. "So hard up for a day off, you go and get bonked on the head."

Garner smiled. "I'd love to be anywhere but here."

"How are you feeling?"

"I got a good sized knot and my head hurts, but otherwise I'm fine."

"I'm surprised Bart could sneak up on you like that." Virgil laughed. "You must be getting old."

"I feel old." Judge looked away. "My mind was on Ida and the mess she's in. I wasn't paying attention, that's the only reason he got the best of me."

"Ida's fine and Ethan told me her mother was at your house with her daughters."

"Good, I've instructed my maid to see that they have everything they need."

Virgil sat in the chair beside the bed. "What's going to happen to Ida?"

"I'm turning it over to the County Judge in Carthage. He'll make the decision."

"Why?"

"I've known her for years. Been friends as long as I can remember. I don't think it would be fair for me to preside over this case. It's too personal."

"I don't understand. You know everyone in town and it never stopped you from passing judgement."

"Ida's different. There's a conflict of interest."

"How so?"

"I'd do everything in my power to keep her out of prison. And that means I'd look the other way when I shouldn't. So, it's best Judge Harvey Hornsby takes over. He's a good man and will see that justice is done."

Virgil reached for his hat, preparing to leave. "Even if that means Ida goes to jail?"

"If that's what the law decides, I'll do all I can to get her an early release."

Virgil shook his head. "I better get going. I have a few things to do before bedtime. Do you want me to contact Judge Hornsby or will you?"

"I'll do it tomorrow."

Virgil stuck his hands in his back pockets. "Do you have a problem with me allowing her to join her mother and daughters at your home tonight?"

A grimace of pain flashed across the judge's face. "I believe she can be trusted not to leave town."

"Okay, I'll see to it right away."

Stepping out of the judge's room, Virgil saw Cora walking out of a patient's room. "My," she said with a weak smile. "Strange seeing you three times in one day."

"I just came by to check on Arthur and the judge."

"I might be a little late tonight. Will you take care of Jack until I get home? We're a little short-handed."

"Sure," he said, unable to show the slightest measure of pleasure. "We'll fix dinner."

She groaned. "Please don't let it be hot dogs and potato chips."

He couldn't help the slight smile that snuck on his face. "That's my and Jack's favorite meal when I have to cook. Not to mention Pal's, too."

"It's not a very healthy dinner."

He walked toward the exit. "Those who work late can't be too choosy."

He made arrangements for Ida to be taken to the judge's house. If Ethan thought it strange, he didn't say anything. Afterwards, Virgil headed to Cora's to see to Jack. He'd already removed his things but still a heavy sadness settled in his chest. Was this the way it was going to be forever? He was ready to settle down and start a family. Yet Cora stubbornly refused to share whatever she thought prevented them for having a life together.

Damn, he hated all this trouble. Nothing else mattered to him. Only having her as his wife and Jack as his son. Why couldn't she see that?

He started dinner determined not to argue with her about their relationship. That always led to her pulling away and them both being miserable. Instead, he'd call Batcher tomorrow and see if he had any news.

CHAPTER EIGHTEEN

The next morning Cora woke to a quiet house and a deep sense of loneliness. Virgil left soon after dinner with the excuse he had a stack of paperwork to do, but she knew he wasn't happy.

She didn't want that to be the case. If only all the things done to her in prison could be washed from her brain. If her fear of men could be smoothed away, if only the sheer thought of being with a man didn't horrify her.

Jack seemed to pick up on her mood. He couldn't find his shoes then he spilled his milk. Realizing the little boy was worried, Cora leaned over and placed a smacking kiss on his cheek and hugged him to her. Jack scrubbed his cheek and grinned. Grabbing his books, he left for school with Maggie and Tommy while Cora went to work.

She saw the judge as he was being released. "I've sent Ida to Carthage for Judge Hornsby to decide what should be done. I want to thank you for letting her clean up at your home."

"That was nothing. I'm glad I could offer her some comfort." She touched his arm. "Let me know if there's anything I can do."

"I will."

As he left, she felt deep sadness for all the things the family had been through. Especially, the children.

GERI FOSTER

She went through the rest of her day thinking of nothing but Virgil. How much she missed his smile, him and Jack laughing and the feel of his lips on hers. He hadn't argued with her last night. Instead, after dinner he cleared the table and left. She missed him immediately, but with everything that had happened lately she knew he was exhausted.

At last Friday came, she was so glad tomorrow would be her day off and she could catch up on her sleep. By three in the afternoon she couldn't help herself, Cora called Virgil. "Hello, are you busy?"

"No, what do you need?"

"I was wondering if you'd like to come to dinner." The silence had her chewing on the eraser at the end of a pencil. "I know we talked about you not sleeping at my house but that doesn't mean I don't miss you."

"I know that, Cora and I miss you too. I'm just trying to stay within the boundaries you've set."

"I know it's difficult and I want to thank you very much for understanding."

"Don't go giving me any gold medals yet."

"You're very sweet."

"Hey, your neighbor struck again."

"What?"

"Today Earl escorted Ervin's father, Jim Butcher, to the judge's chamber. He openly admitted that he hated that Ida killed his son, but according to his own daddy, Ervin deserved what he got. He knew his son had been mistreating his family for years."

"What did the judge say?"

"He released her. The judge dismissed the case on grounds of assault, self-defense and endangerment of a child."

"So, she's free?"

"It all happened right before Ida and I were about to leave for Carthage. Next thing I know, I'm releasing her into the judge's custody should anything come up later."

"I didn't know you could do that."

"I think there's something between Ida and the judge. I don't know what, but he's moved her and her two girls into his home."

"What? That is strange."

"He claimed the shack Butcher provided wasn't fit for pigs."

"I'm so glad that's all straightened out. I'm especially thankful for her daughters."

"They'll be well cared for now."

"So, are you coming for dinner?"

"Why don't I take you and Jack out? It's been a helluva week."

"I agree. See you after work."

Cora felt better about her and Virgil's relationship now that she knew he wasn't mad. Disappointed, but not angry. Also, she was glad Ida Butcher didn't have to look at a life behind bars. No one deserved that. Not for shooting a horrible man who beat you and your children.

She arrived home from work to find Maggie heading toward her house. "Do you mind if Jack spends the night? Briggs and the older boys want to start a fire outside and roast marshmallows tonight."

"Jack would love that." Cora smiled. "I'll return the favor by having Tommy over Saturday night."

"Deal." Maggie turned to go then stopped and looked back over her shoulder. "By the way, how is work?"

"I'm really enjoying it. It's smaller than the hospital I worked at in St. Louis, but I like that better."

"Good, we'll talk tomorrow."

Cora unlocked the door and stepped inside to change clothes before Virgil arrived. There would just be the two of them and she liked the thought of having him all to herself. Lately, so much had happened, she felt a strain between them that worried her.

She'd no sooner fluffed up her hair when Virgil tapped on the door, then used his key to enter. "Are you guys ready?"

"Jack's at Maggie's tonight roasting marshmallows after dark."

"Oh, that sounds like fun." He smiled and her heart melted. "Did we get invited?"

She shook her head. "No such luck."

"Well, where would you like to go? We have time to drive into Joplin if you'd like."

She smiled. "That sounds like fun. I'd like to get out of town for a few hours."

"I know what you mean. I feel like we've been trapped like a hostage since the epidemic."

"That's the truth."

"How's Arthur?"

"He's doing much better. I think he'll be released Monday."

"I bet he'll be good and ready by then."

"Nobody enjoys being in a hospital."

As they left Gibbs City behind them, Virgil turned on the car radio and they listened to Hank Williams sing. Cora looked out at the evening sky. It was cold and winter was coming on fast, but she really enjoyed being outside.

"I'm glad Bart wasn't able to do any more damage than he did. His intention was to kill us all."

Cora shivered. "It's difficult to even think about it."

Virgil chuckled. "Good old Carl saved the day."

She turned to Virgil. "I honestly think Carl should get a commendation for his bravery."

Virgil smiled. "I'm sure he will. But right now, Gibbs City is coming up with one for you and all your hard work when influenza hit the town."

"Me? There were six other people in the church working just as hard as I was."

"I'm sure they'll be mentioned, but you were the one who pulled us all through it."

"Luck had a lot to do with that."

They arrived in Joplin and Virgil drove to a nice restaurant called The Catfish Place. "Best fried catfish in four counties," Virgil said. "But they have a full menu."

"I love catfish."

He looked surprised. "You do?"

"Yes, it's my favorite."

"Well, Jack and I will have to go fishing and catch you some. Do you know how to cook it?"

She smiled as they entered the restaurant. "What do you think?"

They had an enjoyable dinner but Cora felt a strain between them. She reached out and touched his hand. "Virgil, I don't want you to be angry because I've asked you to move out."

"I'm not angry."

"I want you to know that I'm trying to work through some things and when I feel comfortable enough, you and I will have a long conversation."

He smiled. "Just don't stop loving me while you're trying to figure out reasons for us not to be together."

"That isn't what's on my mind and you know it."

On the way home, Cora thought about her feelings for Virgil and why she let the horrible things that happened to her in prison deprive her of living a normal life. That was all behind her now and nobody could make her relive it. It was time to let it go because Virgil deserved better.

When they arrived at her house it was still early and she invited him in for coffee. As she put the pot on the stove, he came up and wrapped his arms around her. "You know, you smell so good."

Her cheeks heated. "Thank you."

She turned and they faced each other with her hips pressed against the kitchen counter. He leaned down and captured her mouth in a kiss that left her dizzy and uncertain. His mouth was hot and demanding in a masculine way and Cora deepened the kiss.

Before she knew it, desire flared inside her and she wanted this man more than anything in the world. She broke the kiss. "Virgil, I want you to make love to me."

His blue eyes stared at her intently. "Are you sure?" He wiped his thumb across her lips. "I don't want you to do something that serious to try to please me. It's all up to you."

"No, you're the man I want."

She turned off the burner then Virgil swung her up in his strong arms and carried her to the bedroom where he gently deposited her on the bed. Lying beside her, he carefully unbuttoned her dress and captured her mouth.

As he slowly removed her clothes, Cora wondered why she'd ever feared this man.

CHAPTER NINETEEN

Virgil woke to the sweet scent of Cora's hair, so he buried his face deeper while reaching around to cup both her bare breasts. Last night had been the most wonderful thing that'd ever happened to him.

He'd known before he loved her, last night he learned just how much. She snuggled deeper into the cover and mumbled. He ran his hand down her bare thighs and kissed the back of her neck.

She rolled over and smiled up at him, her hands roaming freely over his naked body. "You keep doing that and you're going to end up on your back again."

She giggled. "That's where I spent most of the night, if you remember."

He chuckled. "Oh, I'll never, ever forget." Leaning down he captured her mouth in a lusty kiss then he heard the pounding on the back door and Pal barking. With a groan, he sat up. "Who's that?"

Cora pulled the blankets up tighter. "I don't know, but we can't be found like this."

Virgil was already putting on his pants when Jack's voice carried to the bedroom. "Aunt Cora, it's me and Tommy. We want our special chocolate chip pancakes."

"Yeah," Tommy yelled. "Open up."

Virgil slipped on his shirt then glared down at her. "You and those damn chocolate chip pancakes."

She laughed. "Hurry up and let them in before they either knock down the door or freeze to death."

Virgil glanced back just as Cora stretched her arms above her head, allowing the blanket to puddle in her lap. He'd never seen anything sexier.

Opening the door in his bare feet, Virgil quickly ushered the boys inside. "You two are up early."

"It's chocolate chip pancake day. Of course we're up early."

"And Maggie doesn't know how to fix those kinds of pancakes?"

"Naw," Tommy said. "She just makes the plain ones."

Soon Cora came out of the bedroom dressed in a cute day dress with her curly hair piled high on her head. She looked beautiful. She grabbed the boys quickly then bent down and kissed Jack and Tommy on the cheeks. "I didn't expect you boys this morning. I thought you'd eat breakfast at Tommy's house."

Jack held out his hands, trying to explain. "But it's Saturday."

Cora stole a private glance at Virgil. "I'll remember that next time."

"So will I," Virgil grumbled, as he made his way to the bathroom. "And remember I want regular, old, boring flapjacks."

After shaving quickly then sitting on the edge of the bed while he put on his work boots, Virgil looked at the rumpled bed and thought about last night and making love to Cora.

Only the smell of coffee could lure him away. He wanted to crawl right back between the sheets with her and stay there all day. But, he had to deal with "special pancakes", instead.

He went into the kitchen, bent down and kissed Cora on the mouth then poured them both a cup of coffee. While she flipped the boys' pancakes, Virgil enjoyed his first cup of coffee. It wasn't long before he had his own stack of pancakes to enjoy.

As soon as the boys' bellies were full, they ran to play in Jack's room, Pal nipping at their heels. Virgil and Cora ate their breakfast slowly and enjoyed the morning.

The pleasant breakfast was interrupted when Maggie knocked at the door. "I'm sorry they woke you guys so early. I had no idea they were headed here until they yelled out something about special pancakes and it being Saturday."

"It's a thing here. Jack loves chocolate chip pancakes, so we have them every Saturday."

"I could've made them if they'd asked."

"You know how boys are."

Maggie didn't stay long. At the door, she stopped and said, "Don't forget today is Ronnie's birthday and Susan has planned him a very special party."

"I remember. Jack bought him a truck. He's excited to finally get to go to a birthday party."

"He's never been to one before?"

"No, that wasn't something my parents thought he needed. But he'll enjoy himself. Are you dropping Tommy off?"

"Yes, and I thought if it was okay with you, I'd take Jack, too."

"Okay, then I'll pick them up with it's over."

Maggie walked out the door. "Sounds good."

Virgil took Cora's hand. "I really enjoyed last night."

She smiled and turned pink. "I did too."

"So, when are we getting married?"

She blinked and leaned back. "What?"

"Marriage, as in husband and wife."

"We don't have to do that right away."

"What if you're pregnant?"

She swallowed and looked away. "I'm not. That isn't something you need to be concerned about."

"I am. I'm not going to subject you to any more town gossip. We're getting married."

"But I'm not pregnant."

"I know you're a doctor and all, but how do you know?"

"I, I,..." She glanced away and buried her face in her shaking hands. "I can't have children."

That didn't make any sense to him at all. If she'd never been married before, how did she know something like that? He knew there had been men at the prison, but just because she didn't get pregnant by them didn't mean she couldn't carry his child.

"Look, I know about some of the things that went on in that place. While in St. Louis I learned about the prostitution and all that." He captured her hands. "It doesn't matter. But you can't assume because nothing happened before it won't now."

Looking at him, tears filled her eyes and her lips trembled. "I can promise you that I'll never have children."

She stood up and leaned dejectedly against the kitchen sink. Virgil couldn't understand. What was wrong that prevented her from having children?

"That doesn't matter, Cora. I love you and want you to be my wife."

She turned to him. "You deserve more than I can give you, Virgil. You're a wonderful person who deserves a family and a wife without a past."

Before he could answer, the phone rang. "Hello."

"Virgil, it's Batcher."

"What's up?"

"Becker is on his way to arrest Cora. He has a warrant from a judge saying she has to spend an additional month in jail."

"What judge?"

"Judge Milford Blackwell. The same one that sent her to prison in the first place. Contact Judge Garner and see what he can do. No matter what, don't let them put Cora back in that prison if you ever want to see her alive again."

He hung up and turned to Cora. "Get Jack dressed for the birthday party and send him over to Maggie's. We have to leave the house."

"Why?"

Virgil called Ethan. "Get to the station as soon as you can. Hell's coming to town."

Hanging up, he turned to look at her. "Becker is on his way to take you back to prison."

CHAPTER TWENTY

Cora dropped the skillet and froze. She couldn't move, couldn't think and couldn't speak. Becker was coming to get her? How could that happen? What could she do?"

Jack.

Dear God she'd be away from him. That would crush him and her. "Virgil, you have to help me."

"I will. Do what I say. Get Jack dressed, wrap the present then I'll take the boys to Maggie's."

"What if he somehow manages to make me return? What will happen then? Virgil, that man wants me dead."

He grabbed her by the arms. "I'm not going to let that happen. Now, get Jack safely out of harm's way and let's get out of here before it's too late."

She flew into action. Looking at her, Jack paled. Seeing his expression she hugged him against her and tried to reassure him everything was fine. Blinking back tears, she managed a shaky smile. Would this be the last time she'd ever hold him? See him?

Why was this happening?

In a matter of minutes, Virgil was dashing across the street to Maggie's with the boys while Cora nervously straightened the house to keep busy until he returned. She didn't know why it was so important she leave her house tidy, but she knew at the moment she wasn't thinking straight.

Virgil sailed through the back door with Earl trailing right behind him. "What's going on?"

"Becker is on his way to take Cora back to prison."

"The hell he is."

"I don't have time to explain, but we have to get to the office and meet up with the judge. Ethan has contacted him to see if we have any other options."

Virgil helped her with her coat and they ran out the front door. He practically wrecked the car on his way to the town square, but he finally got them there safely.

Ethan had a shotgun in his hand as he held the door open. As soon as they entered, he bolted the door and pulled the curtains so no one could see in. "Judge's on his way."

"Okay, let's wait."

Virgil helped Cora sit in a chair in his office while they prepared to barricade the place shut. Cora couldn't sit still. Jumping up from the chair, she faced the men. "Virgil, I can't let you or Ethan do anything illegal to keep me from going back there. It's not right. I won't do it."

"We're not doing anything wrong. I mean, what if I've already arrested you? They don't have the authority to take a prisoner away from me."

"But you didn't."

"Let's just wait for the judge."

It didn't take long for Judge Garner to come through the door waving a folder in his hand. "Who told you Becker was on the way to get her?"

"Batcher. Said he saw the papers on his captain's desk."

"Did he tell you what kind of papers?"

"No, just to prepare for a showdown."

"Well, we'll no doubt have one if he's that determined to arrest her."

"Is it legal?"

"I can't say until I know what tactic Becker plans to use."

"No matter what he says, I won't let her go. You need to understand that, Judge. I won't let them take her away only to shut her up."

The judge held out his hands. "Now be reasonable. Let's see what we're up against before we start making threats."

"That's not a threat. I'm not giving her up."

Ethan cocked the shotgun. "And I'm the man backing him."

Before Cora could try to reason with Virgil, the squeal of tires filled the air.

Virgil took down a shotgun and loaded it. "Unlock the door."

Ethan slipped the bolt and stood back, the shotgun ready. Becker, Herbert Grubber and Marcus Dennard walked into the sheriff's office like they owned the place. Cora's body literally shook uncontrollably.

Becker hooked his thumbs on his belt. "I see you brought her here for me to pick up and take back to St. Louis."

The judge stepped forward and held out his hand. "Show me what you have there. As far as we're concerned, you aren't taking her anywhere."

JJ burst into the office to stand beside Cora and put his arm around her shoulder. "What's going on? As Miss Williams' attorney, nobody's doing anything without my knowledge."

"I have an order from Judge Milford Blackwell in St. Louis. Says Cora Williams is to be returned to the Missouri State Penitentiary for Women until she's served her full sentence."

JJ lifted a paper in the air. "I have a signed release form that states that Cora Williams served her full term and was released. The only restriction was that she couldn't leave the state of Missouri for one year and she had to notify the law she was in town."

Becker sneered. "You might as well take that to the toilet the next time you take a shit, for all the good it is."

JJ looked at the paper. "It's signed by your head guard, Herbert Grubber."

"I didn't know she was getting out early," the guard tried to defend his actions.

JJ put his hand on his hip. "Isn't it your job to know these things?"

"Blackwell wants her back in prison."

Virgil stepped closer. "Does he want her back in prison, or do you?"

Becker shook his head and grinned. "Doesn't matter, it's the law." He motioned to Herbert. "Put the shackles on her and let's get this over with."

Virgil stepped between the guard and Cora. He pointed the shotgun at the guard's chest. "You're not taking her anywhere unless you can walk through a bullet."

"You're obstructing justice, Sheriff. I can take your badge for that."

Virgil grinned. "Come and get it."

Becker didn't look like he wanted to do that. The longer he stood there, the more uncomfortable he appeared. Cora knew he wanted her handcuffed and in the back of a car heading for St. Louis. A destination she'd never reach.

"You take me in, Becker," Cora said. "And before I leave, before witnesses, I'll put in writing everything that happened in that prison."

When Becker looked doubtful, she stepped closer. "My attorney will take that information and you'll rot in prison." She folded her arms. "I wonder how long a warden would last behind bars, surrounded by prisoners who hate him and want him dead. Just think of all the things they could do to you before they let you die."

Becker paled. "Dammit, I said arrest her and let's get out of here."

Earl burst through the door waving an official looking document. "Got it." He handed the paper to the judge.

After a moment, Judge Garner patted Earl on the back and smiled. Looking at Becker he said. "This is a Protective Order from the United States Attorney General placing Cora Williams in the custody of Sheriff Virgil Carter."

Earl shoved an envelope at Becker. "This, asshole, is a summons to appear in court in five days. You, your prison, and all your guards are under investigation by the DA."

"I can't believe this," Becker shouted. "You should've been smart and just turned her over. Judge Blackwell isn't going to do anything to me."

Judge Garner looked up. "You're not appearing in front of your friend. It's going to be the Honorable Jacob Steinberg." The judge lowered his head and trapped Becker with a menacing glare. "And he's not in anyone's pocket."

"Oh, I forgot," Earl said, with a chuckle. "This here is a warrant for Virgil to arrest Warden Becker and anyone accompanying him."

"What?" Becker sputtered. "You can't be serious."

Virgil smiled. "I think you've met your match, Becker."

CHAPTER TWENTY-ONE

While JJ and Earl guarded Cora, Virgil put Becker and the two other men in the one small, jail cell the county owned. He called Batcher and notified him to make arrangements to escort the prisoners back to St. Louis where they were to be held until the court date.

Unfortunately, Cora was also served with a summons to appear in court as a witness. On the drive to her house, she shook with misery. "I can't testify."

"You threatened to when they were going to take you back to St. Louis."

"But that was just a bluff. I wasn't really going to do it."

"Now the court has demanded you comply". He stopped in front of her house. "You know as long as Becker is able, he'll come after you. He wants you dead. I have no doubt, if he'd been able to get his hands on you today, by now you wouldn't be breathing."

She nibbled her lip. "I know that. But, to tell the whole truth would stir up more trouble and make it harder for me and those trapped inside."

"How can you say that?"

"Honestly, Virgil do you think there is even a remote chance we'll win this?"

He nodded. "I do."

"Have you forgotten about Judge Martin, his son? Even my own father will be against us. These are men with power and money who deal in bribes, coercion, and murder."

"I believe in the truth."

"It took me five years to learn there is no truth, only pain and suffering for those who look too hard for it." She turned to him, her eyes narrowed in accusation. "And now you're going to put me through hell all over again."

Cora got out of the car and shut the door. He wanted to run after her and convince her that justice still worked, and that everything wasn't corrupt and dirty.

He stayed until Cora closed the door behind her, then he drove to his office. He planned to stay close by until Becker was safely out of his county. No telling the things the man was capable of. Sitting in his office, he restlessly drummed his fingers against the desk. Earl came in with a pie in his hand.

"Where'd you get that?"

"Missy."

He dropped back in his chair. "I'm glad you were the one asking. I don't think she'd give me the time of day."

"Oh, you're just griping to hear your head rattle."

"She's mad at me, Earl. Why isn't she mad at you? You're the one that got the Attorney General involved. Speaking of that, how'd you manage to get that done so quickly?"

Earl poured a cup of coffee, took down a chipped, white saucer and cut himself a piece of pie. Sitting on the opposite side of Virgil's desk, he cut into the pie and moaned. "Lordy, that woman can cook."

Virgil helped himself to coffee and pie before returning to his seat. "How'd you get her to give you a pie?"

"I just asked. Told her I was coming down here to help you guard the crooks and I sure could use a peach pie to hold me over."

Virgil groaned and shook his head in disbelief. "And she just gave it to you? Just like that?"

Earl nodded. "Told me to be careful and not to stay the night here." He faked a cough. "My health, you know."

"You're the biggest faker I know, Earl Clevenger." Virgil took a bite of pie. "You're no more sick than I am." He pointed the fork at Cora's neighbor. "And don't tell me you don't like that Miss Winters hanging around, because you do."

"Now don't go getting ahead of yourself. Evelyn can't cook worth a nickel. Why, I'm surprised I'm still alive. But she is kindly." He giggled like a teenager. "She does keep me on my toes."

"I'm glad someone does."

"Hell fire, man. You have to learn how to handle women. You let them think you're interested and the next thing you know, they start playing hard to get. I got no time for that."

"Okay, I don't want courting advice from you. But, tell me how you got Cora out of this mess, not to mention Becker and his cronies in jail."

Earl finished his pie and drained his cup. "I ain't giving up all my secrets, but I will say, do whatever you can for everyone you know. This way, when you need a favor, it makes it hard for them to say no."

Earl left and Virgil watched the elderly man make his way down the street. Leaning his head back, he realized what a difficult day they'd had. An hour ago, he would've believed before the day was out he had to choose between killing a man or letting Cora go. Thank God he didn't have to do either.

While Cora had fears about marriage, he did as well. He dreaded every night he'd wake up from a nightmare and scare her and Jack silly. But, so far his dreams had been shorter and milder while at her house. They still happened, but not as bad.

Ethan entered the office holding up several paper bags. "The prisoners' dinner." He grinned. "I hope they choke on it."

Virgil laughed, "Batcher will be here soon and they'll be off our hands. If it wasn't against the law, I'd let them starve."

"Would serve them right." Ethan nodded toward the bags. "This should be punishment enough. While at Betty's Diner, I ordered the chicken and dumplings."

Virgil's face stiffened and his shoulders shook with laugher. "They'll pay for that, all right."

Ethan came back empty-handed. "They're chowing down. Hope they don't get sick until they reach St. Louis."

"Everyone in town knows to never order that at Betty's Diner. It's just not healthy."

"I know, that's why I insisted."

"Did the waitress look at you funny?"

"Naw, Patty just asked who I was mad at."

"Well, it won't be our problem for much longer."

Ethan eased back on the edge of Virgil's desk. "You think Cora's going to get over being mad at you anytime soon?"

"I don't know. She still doesn't want to testify and I can't say I blame her, but the truth has to come out."

"We don't know what all she's been through, so we can't judge. But looking at those bullies, I can imagine it wasn't pretty."

"No, it wasn't." Virgil nodded at the chair across his desk. "You should've seen her the first time she walked into this office. I swear she was shaking so badly I thought she'd faint."

"I can understand why."

"Me too, now. That day, I remember I never felt so sorry for a woman in all my life."

Ethan stared at Virgil. "It's terrible."

"And when I went to St. Louis, I learned it was all rigged against her. There's no reason why she should have spent one day in jail. Not one."

"Makes you wonder why her father let that happen."

"I can't figure that out. And don't be surprised if he shows up here threatening her. He's that lowly and despicable."

Ethan narrowed his eyes. "I see him in town, I'll make sure he gets shown the way back to St. Louis."

"I'm wondering if the judge can protect her by making her father stay away."

"I don't know enough about the law to figure that out. I always wanted to, but with a wife and three kids, I never had time."

Virgil was surprised. "You wanted to be a lawyer?"

"I wanted to own Big Jim's place. I always dreamed that one day I'd buy it and live in that house like a king. Becoming a lawyer was the practical side of me."

"You're still a young man, Ethan."

"Yeah, with three kids and no wife."

They turned when the door opened and Caroline Dixon walked in with a basket in one hand, Ethan's youngest child, Lizzy, balanced on her hip. "I'm sorry to disturb you two, but I fried up some chicken because I knew you'd be tied up here through dinner."

She handed Ethan the basket. He put it on the desk and took Lizzy. "You didn't have to do that, Caroline. We'd have been okay." He tickled his daughter under the chin to make her giggle.

Caroline smiled timidly. "I didn't mind at all."

She stepped back and folded her hands, her eyes downcast, her cheeks rosy. Virgil looked at Ethan and then back at Caroline and wondered why the two hadn't ever gotten together.

Ethan handed Lizzy back to Caroline and put his hands in his back pockets. "You taking her to my mother's?"

"Yes, I kept her last night, but tomorrow I have too much to do."

"I really appreciate all the help you give my mother."

"Well, I know her health isn't that good, and Lizzy's a very active child."

Ethan smiled. "Yes, she is." He looked into the basket. "As soon as the detective gets here and picks up the prisoners I'll be heading home for the night."

"Good, maybe you can get some sleep."

She turned to leave. "Don't worry about the basket. I'll pick it up tomorrow."

The peach pie earlier had spoiled Virgil's appetite, but Ethan was hungry enough for both of them. He filled a plate, got a cup of coffee and sat down at John's old desk and ate.

Virgil missed his deputy. Missed his company and his friendship. When he told John's folks he'd died, they'd nearly collapsed. The quarantine had prevented them from being with him in the end. An only child, he was their whole life. His father was a carpenter and did some great work but he'd retired years ago. Virgil hoped they could somehow find peace.

About the time Ethan finished eating, Batcher came through the door with two burly deputies. "I'm here to pick up the prisoners."

Virgil stood and shook hands. "They're all yours."

"I can't for the life of me figure out how you managed to pull this off."

"Let's just say Cora has a very influential friend."

"She'll need one. I'm taking these guys back to St. Louis but I heard their lawyer is already working on getting bail set, so they may not stay locked up very long."

"I better not see them in my county or they're dead."

"Let's just hope Judge Martin won't use his influence and that their lawyer can't get the trial moved back."

"I'm hoping, since the Attorney General is involved, none of that will happen."

Batcher cuffed him on the arm. "Hell, we both know this is bigger than we ever imagined."

"I know, and I'm going to see if I can't get to St. Louis and make a few more inquires."

"I've been banging on doors since you left and I've learned you can't squeeze blood out of a turnip."

"No hint of what these guys are up to?"

"Nothing, and I've had a man on Williams since you left hoping he'd lead us to something. We haven't come up with a thing yet."

"We will." He looked at the two deputies. "Let's get these men secured and on the road."

"I brought extra backup. One never knows with these men. Harvey is waiting in the car with a loaded shotgun if anyone makes the wrong move."

"Good, save the taxpayers some money."

Virgil unlocked the cell and helped Batcher escort the subdued prisoners out the door. Once they were securely inside the vehicles, Virgil leaned down. "Come into my county again and I'll kill you without asking why you're here."

CHAPTER TWENTY-TWO

After Earl left with the peach pie, Cora nervously paced the floor of her living room. Virgil had no idea what he was asking her to do. It was one thing to threaten and quite another to actually do the deed.

After doing dishes, laundry, and scrubbing the floor, Cora changed the sheets. Oh, the things she and Virgil had done between them the night before was enough to scald her cheeks.

Sitting at the kitchen table she thought about how close she came to going back to prison today. Wringing her hands, she wondered if she'd get out of this alive and, if anything should happen to her, what would become of Jack. Suddenly she had the urge to straighten out her future.

She picked up the phone and asked for the Sheriff's office. When Virgil answered the phone he sounded relieved it was her. "I just want to ask you something."

"Okay."

"If anything happens to me I want you to promise you'll take care of Jack." She whisked the tears from her cheeks.

"Cora, nothing is going to happen to you. I won't let it."

"But if it does, I need to know he's loved, cared for and safe."

"How can you think I wouldn't?"

"I need to hear the words, Virgil. You need to promise me."

"I swear I'll raise Jack as my own son as long as I'm alive."

"Thank you."

"Cora, this is all going to work out. You'll see. There's no reason to worry and no reason to expect the worst."

"I just have to know Jack's safe."

"He will be."

"Good." She hung up the phone then put on her coat to go pick Jack and Tommy up from Ronnie's birthday party. Leaving the house, she cautiously looked up and down the street before stepping off the porch.

Virgil thought with Becker and the others locked up she was safe. He didn't know the warden's reach. She did, but the sheriff didn't have a clue. If he had, he would've killed Becker where he stood because that's the only way to stop him.

She plastered on a smile before ringing the Welsh's doorbell and was surprised when Ronnie answered and jumped into her arms. She hugged him tightly. "My, what a big boy you've become."

"I'm six now, Aunt Cora." He held up an open palm and one finger. "I'm all grown up."

She set him down and knelt in front of him. "You're such a handsome lad. You're going to have all the girls chasing you around the school yard."

"I don't want no girls. I want to be a cowboy."

Susan came in. "This has been a very remarkable day for him. I think he'll be asleep before his head hits the pillow. I know I will."

"They can be exhausting."

"That's true, but he had so much fun today. All his little friends came and they laughed and played games all afternoon."

"That's what birthday parties are all about."

"Won't you come in and have a cup of coffee?"

"No, I'd better get these two buckaroos home."

"Thank you for letting them come."

"Always."

Susan pulled Cora into her arms and whispered, "Thank you so much for giving us a chance to love Ronnie."

"You're more than welcome. I've never seen him happier."

After much moaning and groaning, Jack and Tommy finally put their coats on and she had to practically drag them away from the party. Outside, the two boys were so excited they could barely contain themselves. They ran, hopped, skipped and jumped all the way. It would be a while before Jack would settle down enough to go to sleep.

After dropping Tommy off and convincing Maggie that nothing happened earlier, Cora rushed home. As soon as they walked in the back door, Virgil came in the front.

Jack ran to him, filled with excitement. "Ronnie's birthday was the most fun I've ever had. We played games, ate birthday cake, won prizes and tried to pin a tail on a donkey while we had a blindfold on."

"Wow, that must be really hard to do."

"It was, but Tommy came the closest."

"Good for him." Virgil sat on the couch and Jack climbed up in his lap. "Did Ronnie like the present we picked out of him."

"Yeah, he said it was his favorite."

"Then we did good."

"I'll say."

Jack crawled down from Virgil's lap and turned on the radio. Cora and Virgil shared a troubled glance. "Are you hungry?"

"No, Earl brought me a piece of peach pie."

"We have peach pie?" Jack perked up. "Can I have some?"

"No young man. You've had enough sugar today." She looked at Virgil. "I felt the least I owed Earl was a peach pie."

"He thoroughly enjoyed it. I'm surprised he offered me a piece."

"He's quite the mystery man."

"You're telling me."

Cora stayed in the kitchen fidgeting with a dish towel. "I swear he's Superman."

"Yeah, if he just had a costume."

"I'm sorry I called you about Jack, but I had to know. I had to come to terms with the fact that no matter what happens, he'd be okay."

He sat Jack in the corner of the couch and came to stand in front of her. Taking her hand, he placed it on his heart. "I know you think I'm a small time sheriff who's never dealt with the big leagues in St. Louis. I can even understand. But don't ever underestimate me."

He caressed her cheek and gazed into her eyes. "People in the past who have, aren't here to talk about it. I know Becker's bad. I know he can get someone to come here and hurt you. I know he wants to shut you up and will stop at nothing." He lifted her chin. "I'm just as determined to protect you as he is to destroy you."

"Then I hope you win. But don't expect me to be grateful or willing to go through with this plan. I never wanted any of this."

"I've learned in this life, good usually triumphs over evil. Not every time, but most of the time."

CHAPTER TWENTY-THREE

The last five days had been tense for Virgil. He had practically no sleep the entire time because he wanted to keep Cora safe. She'd been cordial, but distant and distracted. Tomorrow morning they would leave for St. Louis. He hadn't had a chance to leave town sooner because he feared something might happen to Cora and he wanted to be close.

Carl, Buford and Virgil's dad walked into the office. "What are you guys doing here?"

"Don't know. Just got a call from Arthur to meet him this morning," Carl said. "We don't have any idea what it's about."

Arthur walked in, his arm still in a sling. "Morning men. I hope I didn't take you away from anything important."

Carl shuffled his feet. "We're okay. What'd you need?"

"I've learned that you're in the process of trying to get a GI loan for a business here in town."

"That's right," Virgil's dad said. "They're trying to buy my old gas station."

"I've called you here to tell you I've cancelled the loan application and I'll gladly finance your business."

Carl shook his head. "You don't have to do that, Arthur. We might get the money."

Arthur raised his hand. "You might, but there's no need. I don't like the service I get from Eddie and Sons so I'll gladly help you open a filling station as long as you always consider the customer first and making money second."

"We'd planned on that," Buford said. "Mr. Carter here made it clear that's the only way to stay in business."

"Good. Do you gentlemen have a figure in mind?"

"We've been working on that." Carl offered. "Between Virgil and his dad we were hoping we wouldn't have to ask for much."

"I want you three to come with me to my office. We'll come up with a business plan and know exactly how much money you'll need to hold you over until you start making a profit." He looked at Virgil's dad. "You, sir deserve a profit. Let's put our heads together and make this happen."

Arthur turned and walked out the door, the other men following behind with big smiles. Virgil thought about how kind Arthur was to be willing to take a chance on two men who needed a break. He didn't have to do that, but they'd be much better off under Arthur's guidance. The man knew how to turn a dime.

Virgil avoided Cora's house because she'd been so unhappy with him, he didn't want to upset her any more. He knew she hated the thought of going to St. Louis and facing Becker, Martin and her father.

Batcher called earlier to say it looked like Williams might be headed this way, but he didn't show. Turned out he had a mistress he'd been neglecting lately.

Virgil would never mention that to Cora, but he wondered how it played into the scheme of things. With Ethan coming in, he walked to the courthouse to see if the judge was busy. He was called in immediately.

"No news if that's why you're here."

Virgil let out a long breath. "I don't know why I'm here. I want to be in St. Louis tailing Judge Martin and Williams, not stuck waiting for someone to find something."

"It doesn't work that way."

"Did Becker and his guards make bail?"

"No, not allowed. Judge Steinberg held firm."

"Are they investigating the prison?"

"I think so, but I don't know what they've found."

"Batcher doesn't know much either. What are we going to do if we get to St. Louis and there's no evidence of any wrongdoing?"

"You and JJ will testify to what you saw when you visited the prison. There's also Cora's information. I have a person inside who's agreed to talk."

"That's all hearsay and you know it."

The judge leaned his head back. "What do you want me to say, Virgil? What do you need to hear so the investigators can do their jobs?"

"I need proof, hardcore proof that no one can dispute."

"That's what everyone's looking for."

"But they haven't found it."

"We still have a little time."

Virgil jumped to his feet. "You can sit here and hope something happens, but I'm going to St. Louis. I'll meet you there tomorrow."

"But what about Cora?"

"I have a dependable guard on her twenty-four hours a day."

"I thought you were driving her to St. Louis tomorrow."

"I'll already be there. She can ride with you."

Virgil stormed out of the judge's office, packed his bag, gave Ethan instructions and left town. He thought about dropping by the hospital and telling Cora but he didn't want to see her right now. What he wanted was some good old-fashioned, hard evidence and an end to Cora's fears.

He called Batcher as soon as he hit town and they made arrangements to meet without anyone knowing. At the diner, Virgil ordered coffee and waited.

It didn't take long for Batcher to show up, his lookout, loitering outside the door. "What are you doing here today?"

"I needed something to get my mind off the trial and nothing would do that better than finding out exactly what those bastards have been up to."

"Every time I think I'm getting close, I get shut down. I know it's coming from Judge Martin, but I've just played it cool because I don't want to get kicked off the investigation all together."

"That's good." Virgil took a sip of coffee. "You know when you told me about Williams' affair I couldn't help but wonder what his wife would think about that."

"Okay, but I get the feeling they don't have much of a marriage. Close as I can tell, it's more for show than anything else."

"It might be, but no woman likes to be made a fool of."

"You're right. However, Williams had been very discrete about the other woman. Seems he goes out of his way to keep his wife and his friends from finding out."

"He probably does. I'm sure he doesn't want to be the topic of local gossip."

"Not with the reputation he's trying to protect. But again, he's keeping it a damn good secret."

Virgil grinned. "Mrs. Williams doesn't know that. And wouldn't she be upset to find out that everyone knows but her?" Virgil winked. "Hell hath no fury like a scorned woman."

CHAPTER TWENTY-FOUR

The dreaded day had finally arrived and Cora could barely dress herself. The nightmare had returned in horrific force. Maggie had offered to watch Jack for as long as the trial lasted, but that did little to ease her mind. Looking around the house, she couldn't help wonder if she'd see it again or would they put her back in prison like Warden Becker threatened?

She'd almost rather die than step foot in that hellhole. But, if the judge decided she had to go back, Cora had all her papers in order. JJ had made out her will and her personal life was in order and locked up tight. Jack would be secure and cared for. That's all she cared about.

Cora jumped at the knock at the door. Looking out first, she breathed a sigh of relief and let Maggie in. "Come on in, do you have time for coffee?"

"Maybe a quick cup. When is Virgil coming to pick you up?"

Cora poured them both a cup then took a seat. "I don't know. I haven't heard from him lately."

Maggie leaned back. "Why not?"

Cora rubbed her forehead. "God only knows. I think he's probably mad at me because things have been so strained I asked him to move out."

"You've done that before and he always comes back around."

Cora looked away. "He wants me to marry him."

Maggie adjusted her chair so she sat directly in front of Cora. "That's the natural progression of things, lady. The man loves you. Why wouldn't he want to marry you? Better yet, why aren't you jumping at the chance to land a man like Virgil Carter?"

"He wants to get married right away."

"So?"

"Like in a matter of days."

Maggie blinked, shook her head then smiled. "Oh, I see now."

"I'm not sure you do, but he has nothing to worry about." She lowered her voice. "I can't have children."

"How do you know that?"

"Trust me. It's not possible."

"Does he know that?"

"Yes, be he refuses to believe me."

Maggie leaned back. "Well, that's a man for you."

Jack and Tommy ran out of the bedroom bundled up and ready to leave. "Thanks for watching Jack. I'll stay in touch."

Maggie hugged her tightly. "You'll be back before you know it."

"I hope so."

Reaching down, Cora pulled Jack into a tight hug. Holding him away from her, she blinked back tears. "No matter what happens, remember that I love you more than anything in the world."

Eyes wide and wary, Jack asked, "Is something wrong, Aunt Cora?"

She smiled. "Nothing's wrong, I'm just going to miss you."

"I'm going to be sleeping in Tommy's bed. After everyone falls asleep, we always make up stories and talk about dragons."

Maggie took the boy's hands and headed for the door. "You only think we're sleeping."

After Maggie and the boys left she didn't know what to do besides wait for Virgil. It wasn't long before the doorbell rang and JJ waited on the porch. "You ready?" he asked.

"Are you driving me to St. Louis?"

"Yes, we'll have time to prep for the trial."

"I thought Virgil would be here."

"He's already there. Left early yesterday."

"Oh, I didn't know that."

Cora wondered what he was doing. Why had he left without telling her and what did he hope to learn? Her nerves grew taut and sweat peppered her palms.

"JJ, do to think they will take me back to prison?"

He started up the car and looked at her. "I'm going to do everything in my power to see that doesn't happen. If we can prove the Warden, Judge Martin and, sorry to say, your father, were up to no good, your whole case could be thrown out."

"I'm so nervous I don't think I can sit in another courtroom and wait while my life is being decided by a bunch of strangers. The stress is enough to make a sane person crazy."

"Now, remember, the prison is what's in question here. Next, were laws broken by other parties, and third does the court deem that you need to finish your thirty day sentence."

"That's a lot to prove in a couple of days."

"It might take longer. But, I think your situation will be dismissed because you were a model prisoner, you never broke any rules and the reason you went to prison in the first place is highly questionable."

"Let's hope you're right."

"We made arrangements where we'll all be staying in the same hotel. This way we can get to court together and no lawyers will be working behind the scenes to cut a deal."

"Cut a deal? Are you kidding? They'd behead me if given the opportunity."

"That's where you're wrong. When a lawyer sniffs out that the situation isn't going in their favor, the first thing that comes to mind is a plea bargain."

"I just want this over with."

JJ reached over and squeezed her hand. "We all do. Remember, you're not alone in this."

They arrived at the hotel and Cora reached for her suitcase from the backseat. Virgil appeared at her side and took it. "I'll show you to your room."

"What have you been doing here?"

"Investigating with Batcher."

"Have you learned anything?"

"We're piecing a few things together."

He led the way up the stairs and stopped at room 206. "This is your room. I'm right next door. Please don't leave the hotel without me or someone with you." He turned the key and shoved open the door.

The room was larger than she expected with a comfortable looking bed. A radio sat on a dresser and two chairs and a table took up the corner. "This is nice," she said. "But I miss Jack already."

"Maggie have him?"

Cora's gazed clashed with Virgil. They talked like strangers. "I wish he'd had the chance to say goodbye to you before you left. He asked about you constantly."

Virgil set down the suitcase and leaned against the wall. "I hope you understand that I couldn't just sit there and wait."

"I try."

"The truth is out there, Cora, and I won't rest until I find out what I need to know to break you free from all this. I don't care how long it takes. I promise you I'll do whatever is necessary."

"I know you will, Virgil."

He turned to leave. "Please don't call your parents and tell them where you're staying. I don't think they need to know."

"Why?"

"I think it's just best if your whereabouts are kept quiet."

Cora lowered her head. "I know my father is a bad man, Virgil. You don't have to protect me from that."

"The problem is, you don't know just how bad he is."

Their gazes met. "Is he involved in this? Did he put Becker up to putting me back in prison?"

"I don't think he did. The warden has enough reasons to want you back under his control. You know too much and he no longer has you where he wants you."

Cora swallowed. "You know if they take me back to the prison they'll kill me, don't you?"

"That's why it's important they don't get their hands on you."

CHAPTER TWENTY-FIVE

Instead of going to his room, Virgil visited the judge's room on the third floor. After being let in, he took the chair closest to the window. "She's here. Scared out of her wits, but they made it."

"Good, did you tell her not to contact her parents?"

"Yes, but I don't think she would anyway because there's a lot of bitterness between them."

The judge took the other chair and leaned back, balancing the chair on its hind legs. "That doesn't mean her lowdown father won't reach out and try to threaten her."

"I was worried about Jack, too. That's why I hired Carl to keep a sharp eye out should anyone decide they want to kidnap him to keep Cora from testifying."

"Good thinking."

"I told Carl, if it looked like anyone was a threat to Jack, to kill them and we'll clean it up later."

The judge stared at him. "You're really getting close to the edge, Virgil. I don't want you to change the person you are for Cora or anyone else. Not even me."

"I don't want her back in prison."

"None of us do, but you're an honorable man. You've always done the right thing. Don't ever lose that."

"You know the easiest thing in the world for her father to do would be to hold Jack hostage. Cora would clam up tighter than a bank vault."

"You're right, but I've put the word out to their attorneys that Jack is under the Attorney General's protection. Anything happens to that boy and someone's ass is going to fry."

"And you talk about me walking the line."

The judge laughed. "Well, I can say what I want. I'm older."

"I heard we're expected in court at eight in the morning."

"We'll be listening to opening arguments. Judge Martin and Williams' attorneys will try to get their cases thrown out of court for lack of evidence and the fact that they had nothing to do with Cora going to jail or her treatment while incarcerated."

"You think the judge will go for that?"

Judge Garner shrugged. "I don't know. When I think what I would do, I'm drawn to the conclusion that I'd want to know all the facts of the trial, exactly what Martin had to do with the death of Eleanor and why Williams let his daughter go to prison."

"But this judge doesn't know all that."

"True and I refuse to meet with him to discuss the case. I want him to be independent and draw his own conclusion."

Virgil let out a tired breath. "That's so risky."

"It's called following the legal system. It works most of the time and it will work this time."

Virgil stood and walked to the door. "I'm meeting up with Batcher in a few minutes. Make sure Cora has dinner."

"When will you be back?"

"Not tonight, for sure. But I'll be in court."

"Have you learned anything yet?"

"We're starting to see the tip of the iceberg."

"Hurry, time's wasting."

Virgil left and slipped into David's unmarked car. He'd checked it out with the excuse he was following a snitch. With any luck, they'd soon lose the officers tailing them.

"I followed that lead we got this morning and you're going to be interested in where it took me."

"Really, I didn't think it held much hope."

"Oh, but it did."

"We know where the Martins are?"

"They're sweating their asses off right now."

"Williams?"

"He's completely clueless and that's exactly the way he's going to stay."

"Yeah, I like that." Virgil grabbed the strap when Batcher took a sharp turn. "Are we headed for the waterfront?"

"I found a guy who's willing to talk for a buck."

"Okay, we'll give him that then the lawyer can subpoena him to court even if it's as a hostile witness."

"We'll need more than him if we want to pull down the whole organization."

"What about that contact in Chicago I turned you on to?"

Batcher looked at him and grinned. "Damn, you're a good judge of character."

Virgil chuckled. "The guy was in my platoon. He's good people."

"He's a goldmine in this case."

"Let's just hope it works out."

"We have to wait for the dock hands to come on the night shift. Want to get a bite to eat?"

"Yeah, I skipped lunch today."

Just as Batcher turned the corner, Virgil noticed that the streets were empty and not a single car was parked in the vicinity. "I'm not liking this, Virgil."

"Me neither. Back up and turn around."

Batcher stepped on the gas and sped down the street backwards. At the first turnoff, he spun the car around and headed toward downtown. Racing as fast as the vehicle would go, Virgil saw a roadblock up ahead.

"They're waiting for us."

"Yeah," Batcher said. "But those aren't cops."

"No, they're not."

Batcher gripped the steering wheel. "You think we can ram them?"

Virgil turned and check behind them. Four cars were on their tail. "We don't have much of a choice."

"Nice to know so many people want us dead."

"That just tells me we're damn good at our jobs."

"Hold on tight." Batcher had the gas pedal all the way to the floor.

The Ford motor strained to keep up with the demand, but they flew down the street quicker than Virgil could count the buildings.

One hand on the dashboard, the other gripping the passenger strap, Virgil ducked just as Batcher slammed into two late model DeSotos.

CHAPTER TWENTY-SIX

Cora cautiously looked through the peephole and saw the judge on the other side before opening the door. "Hello, Judge Garner. Won't you come in?"

"I know it's early, but instead of being stuck up here in your hotel room, how about we go to the lobby and have a cup of tea?"

"I'd love that." She picked up her purse, pressed the front of her dress and hooked her arm though the judge's offered elbow. "I was just thinking this was going to be a very long day."

"I'm sure you'd like nothing better than to hurry up and get it over with."

"I would if I were certain I wasn't going back to prison."

They walked down the stairs, the judge leading the way. "We'll do everything possible to make that not happen."

In the brightly lit anteroom, a nice restaurant decorated in dark mahogany took up the right side of the downstairs lobby, directly across from the check-in counter.

A hostess led them to a nice table in the corner. The judge ordered whiskey and Cora decided on tea for a nice change. "This is very nice."

"Yes, it is. How is your room? Is it to your liking?"

"Why wouldn't it be? The Bellaire is one of the best hotels in St. Louis."

"Good, that's why I picked it. I thought if the city of St. Louis insists we all come here, the least they can do is pay for a nice place for us to stay."

"Is everyone here?"

"Yes, and that includes JJ. He's at the courthouse right now, meeting with the District Attorney."

"I'm glad."

The judge reached over and took her hand. "Relax and think of this as a short vacation. Order room service, have a bottle of fancy wine."

Cora laughed as the tea and several small cakes were set in front of her. "I could never do that." She thought for a moment. "I will admit there was a time I could. When all that meant something. But not anymore."

"You were a very successful doctor with a financially secure future. Why not live an extravagant lifestyle?"

She stirred a spoon of sugar into her cup. "Because it makes you overconfident and you began to think you're above anything bad happening." She bit her bottom lip. "And then it does."

"I'm sure the death of your sister was a terrible experience for you, Cora. To lose a sibling is something you never get over." He took a sip of his liquor. "I lost my brother when he was only nineteen."

Cora leaned forward. "I'm so sorry."

The judge looked away. "It was so silly. He was strong and healthy one minute then laying on the operating table the next."

"What happened?"

"We'd gone hunting with our father. Three men, each were trying to outshoot the other. I fired at a pheasant that flew up out of the brush and my gun misfired." He took another sip. "I opened the barrel to see what was wrong, the shotgun went off and the bullet lodged in my brother's throat."

Cora batted back tears. "I'm so very sorry. It was rude of me to ask."

"It's okay. They tried to save him, but he was dead by the next morning."

"Accidents can happen to anyone, but those that happen to us are the worst."

"Yes, I had no way of making it up to my parents, my brother's fiancée or his friends."

"You must've felt so lonely."

"That word didn't come close to what I felt. I wanted to die myself." He looked up at Cora. "I'd have done it but I knew it would've been the end of my mother and father. I couldn't make them suffer more."

"I'm glad you didn't."

"To this day I miss him terribly and it's been years."

"When my sister died, I felt part of me died, too. The good part of me. She was everything I ever wanted to be."

"But you're a doctor."

"I am, but Eleanor had a way with people I'd never taken the time to cultivate. She was friendly, open, eager to help and genuinely good inside."

"You're all those things, Cora."

"Oh, I wasn't always. I was a snob, a career woman and on the way to being one of the most successful doctors in the United States."

"Then you went to prison."

"No, what changed me was Jack."

"Your nephew?"

"Yes. When I learned Eleanor was dead and that, in my opinion, Dan had murdered her, I was overtaken by anger. I wanted to kill that bastard for what he had taken away from us."

"But you couldn't."

"Somewhere in the rational part of my brain I realized that Jack would need me now. So instead of shooting Dan in the head, I fired at his leg."

"I assume you didn't suspect that would get you arrested."

"I didn't even think Dan had the guts to go to the police and complain because that would bring suspicion back on him."

"So how did you end up in jail?"

"Judge Martin went to the public officials he carries in his pocket and insisted I be arrested. The rest is history."

"They'd been better to just let it go."

"No, they were smart to lock me away."

"Why would you say that?"

"If they hadn't, I would've kept searching until I found what I needed to put Dan Martin away and his father knew it."

"That makes sense."

"Also, I'd long suspected that the Martins weren't on the level when it came to making money. They had no legitimate companies, businesses or employees. Yet they were rich beyond your wildest dreams."

"Something illegal?"

"Of course. And the first thing I did after shooting Dan was hire a private investigator."

"What did he find out?"

"We'll never know. His body was found down by the Mississippi with a bullet between his eyes."

CHAPTER TWENTY-SEVEN

Virgil felt the Ford as it went airborne over the vehicles blocking their way then the hard bounce when they smacked on the cement on the other side. The Ford kept right on going.

"Wow, what a ride," Batcher yelled out. "Come and get us now you sons of a bitch."

"Good driving, David. Remind me to never challenge you to a race."

"They're on to us now," Batcher said. "We need to ditch the car."

"Got any ideas?"

"Yeah," he looked at Virgil and grinned. "I know a guy."

In no time they pulled up to a garage in a neglected neighborhood where a colored man came out and opened the door to allow them to drive inside.

"What the hell are you up to now, Batcher?"

Batcher slid out of the car and grabbed the stranger's hand. "Same old stuff." He slapped him on the back.

"This is Otto Jamison Prince." Batcher turned to Virgil. "This is my partner in crime, Virgil Carter."

"Pleased to meet you, but you wearing a Sheriff's badge. What's you doing hanging around with this crook?"

"I'm not a crook. You and your men don't know how to hold your liquor or play poker."

The men behind them started laughing. "I can't believe you kiss your wife with that lying mouth."

Batcher laughed so hard he had to lean against the Ford. "That's the sound of a man who loses at cards regularly."

"No, that's the sound of a man who knows you're a cheater."

Batcher play punched Otto on the shoulder. "You caught me yet?"

"No, but someday I will."

"Until then, I'm still the king of poker."

"Humph, you're a joke." Otto looked at the car they drove in. "Whatcha got here?"

"It's a police vehicle and we have some guys after us. We need another car and this returned to the station."

"Well," Otto hooted and slapped his thigh. "Is that *all* you want? You sure you don't want a steak dinner and a bottle of fine wine?"

Batcher pulled out a wad of money. "No, you can keep the food and liquor, I just need to move."

Otto motioned them to the far end of the garage. Past several cars under repair, including a police vehicle. He pulled back a tarp that exposed a late model Oldsmobile. "This is the best I got. She's got some miles on her, but she's clean as a whistle."

"We'll take it." Batcher handed Otto several bills and the keys to the Ford. "Take care of that, will you?"

"Yeah, I'll have it dropped off later tonight when it's quiet."

"Thanks, buddy."

The garage door opened and Batcher backed out the Oldsmobile. "Where do you know him from?"

"A couple of detectives in my precinct tried to pin a murder on him and his brother. I knew the case was weak, so I dug a little deeper and found out who was really responsible. We've been friends ever since."

"Those are good friends to have."

"The best."

"Okay, since they don't know what car we're driving, let's eat then head for the docks. I want to wait until it's nice and dark. We get caught down there we'll end up at the bottom of the Mississippi."

"Let's take a little side trip and see if we can recognize anyone at that roadblock. If they're still there. That may be the one big lead that brings all this together."

"Okay, but pull your hat down low, we don't want to be made." Driving, Batcher took off his jacket. "Put this on over your shirt."

Virgil kept an eye out as Batcher drove back toward the roadblock. From a block away, Batcher killed the engine and they walked toward the confusion at the end of the road. No one would suspect them as law enforcement as they neared and turned into an electronics shop.

The owner was staring out the window. "What's going on out there," Virgil asked. "The police looking for someone?"

The paunchy clerk pushing fifty glanced over his shoulder. "There ain't no police cars out there. Don't know who those men think they are blocking the street like that, but I called the cops."

Sirens sounded in the distance. "That must be them," Batcher said. "Maybe they'll get to the bottom of it."

Before the authorities arrived, the bunch was long gone. "Well, as usual the law is a day late and a dollar short in this neighborhood."

"That's too bad. When did you see them blocking the street?"

"Why they did it so fast I didn't know what was happening. But when I heard the gunfire I came back in my shop and shut the door."

"Hum," Virgil said. "Makes one wonder what they were up to."

"No good," the clerk replied. "No damned good, that's for sure."

"How many were there all together," Batcher asked. "I counted five cars."

"What are you the cops?"

Virgil shrugged. "Just curious, that's all. It's not every day you have a shootout and an unauthorized roadblock."

"Yeah, it's like the criminals are taking over the whole damned city." The clerk scratched his huge belly. "I did see one man standing over on the opposite corner. He was dressed in a fancy suit and watching everything."

"Maybe he's in on it."

"He sure the hell wasn't as scared as I was."

Batcher and Virgil bought a few batteries and left the store. They walked to the crime scene but didn't see anything except spent shell casings. The police hadn't even investigated, so they were useless.

Batcher kicked the sidewalk with the toe of his shoes. "I can't help but wonder who's so damned powerful they could manage to block off a city street, have armed gunmen shoot at people and still be able to stand on the corner and watch."

"Did you get that shopkeeper's name?"

"Yeah, I did."

"Good, we might come back later with a picture for him to identify someone."

"Now wouldn't that be sweet?"

CHAPTER TWENTY-EIGHT

Cora went back to her room after visiting with Francis for most of the afternoon. He promised to pick her up for dinner around six.

Looking out her window, she saw St. Louis Memorial Hospital in the distance. Working there felt like a lifetime ago. The days building her career and impressing the right people were over. Now she wanted Jack happy and her friends true and devoted.

Virgil was out there somewhere doing God only knew what, but she hoped he was safe and would come back to her tonight. She missed him more than she'd ever imagined. Also Jack stayed on her mind. If anything happened to him, her life would be over. There'd be no hope of her surviving.

She removed her dress and lay across the bed but couldn't go to sleep. Instead, her mind drifted to all that had happened over the years. Her time in prison, moving to Gibbs City and now this. A new heartache to add to all the others.

Unable to sleep, she called a number she hadn't dialed in five years. Twenty minutes later she was walking down Franklin Street toward a small, but fashionable bistro. She waved when she spotted an old colleague.

Pushing through the door, she weaved through the mostly empty tables to the back to great Dr. Joann Holmes.

"How are you," Joann asked with a smile. "It's so good to see you."

"It's nice to see you too."

"I didn't know you were...," Joann looked away. "Released."

"Yes, I've been for several months now. I can't tell you how wonderful it feels to not be locked up anymore."

"I can imagine."

The waiter came and they both ordered coffee. The tension between them was thick and uncomfortable. Cora forced the smile to remain on her face yet she couldn't ignore the beautiful dress and shoes Dr. Holmes wore, or the expensive, sable coat she had thrown across her arm.

None of that passed her notice. How could it, when everything Joann had should've been Cora's? Only by a strange twist of fate did they end up in reverse roles.

"It looks as if you've done well in my absence."

"I've worked really hard, but we both know that I'm not the doctor you were."

"*Am*. I am a doctor. My license was reinstated."

Joann's smile slipped and she nearly spilled her coffee. "How did you manage that?"

"Oh, it's amazing what can happen when you remember why you became a doctor in the first place."

"We all know that. To help people."

"Do you call doing what you did helpful?"

Joann looked away. "I don't know what you're talking about."

Cora leaned closer. "Shall I remind you?"

Joann stood. "I simply did what I thought was right. I didn't shoot Dan. You did."

"I didn't have an affair with him. You did."

Joann gasped. "That was a long time ago."

"So is five years in prison." Cora stood. "I'll find out how you were involved in the death of my sister and if it turns out your hands are dirty, I'll see you pay."

"I didn't." Pressing her hands to her throat, Joann declared, "I would never hurt anyone."

"Then why did you wait an hour after my sister was shot to call an ambulance?"

The shocked look on Joann's face told Cora that she didn't know that Cora had been discreetly investigating the death of her sister. "How do you know it was an hour?"

"I also know you confronted Eleanor with the affair. That's why she and Dan were arguing."

Joann grabbed Cora's hand. "Dan called me, but I didn't have anything to do with her death. She was dead when I got there."

Cora turned to leave. Glancing over her shoulder she said, "I'll get to the truth, Joann. I usually do because I'm smarter than you and I always have been."

Cora walked away knowing that Joann would run right to Dan if they were still seeing each other, but she didn't care. No one knew where she was staying and, as she neared the hotel, she made sure she hadn't been followed.

JJ stood outside her door, a worried expression on his face. "Where were you?"

"I had to pay a visit to an old friend."

"Are you trying to get yourself killed? Virgil doesn't want your parents to know you're here. He's afraid they'll come and try to intimidate you by threatening you with Jack."

"That won't work." At least she hoped it wouldn't. She didn't think her parents would intentionally hurt the boy.

"You do know Virgil has someone watching Jack every minute. He's not taking any chances."

That relieved her mind more than she'd imagined. "I'm glad to know that, JJ. Leave it to the sheriff to think of everything."

"He has."

"Are we going to dinner?"

"I think it best if the judge and I have dinner with you in your room."

Cora cocked her head. "Why?"

"Because we don't need the attention. And a man of color sitting at a restaurant with a white woman, even an elegant restaurant, isn't acceptable."

"I think that's silly. You're my cousin and I'm very proud of you."

"Good, all the more reason to eat in your room."

A knock sounded and JJ let the judge enter. "Is Virgil joining us?"

"I don't think so. He told me he'd be gone all night but to expect him at court tomorrow."

"Good," the judge said. "Let's order dinner. I'm starving." He pointed at Cora. "And I want you to have a glass of wine. You need to relax. Your face is flushed."

Cora touched her cheeks. "I had a rather heated confrontation with an old co-worker."

JJ looked up from the menu. "I thought she was your friend."

"She was until she had an affair with my sister's husband."

"What?" the judge asked. "Dan Martin was having an affair when your sister was murdered?"

"Yes, I learned when I was in prison."

JJ sat on the edge of the bed. "You found that out while you were locked up?"

Cora nodded. "I was in prison, not in outer space."

The judge took a seat. "Did the authorities suspect anything like that going on?"

"No, but Ted Young did a little investigating on the side for me."

"So, Dan Martin had a motive?"

CHAPTER TWENTY-NINE

Virgil didn't arrive back at the hotel until six the next morning. By the time he'd showered, shaved and dressed, it was time to meet everyone downstairs for breakfast in a small restaurant tucked away in the corner of the lobby.

He almost tripped when he saw Cora. She looked beautiful in a nicely fitted cream suit with matching heels. Her hair formed delicate curls around her face. She smiled up at him and his heart nearly stopped. He loved her so much.

The thought that he might lose her jarred his body so badly he touched the wall to keep upright. No matter what happened, he couldn't let her go. Not now, not after making love to her and claiming her as his.

"Good morning, Virgil," the judge said. "I hope you had a restful night."

Ha, the judge had to be kidding. His eyes were so gritty he hated to blink. He hadn't slept since arriving in St. Louis. However, he and Batcher had dug up a lot of information. If only they could connect everything.

"I'm fine." He took Cora's arm and led her to a nearby table. JJ was already at the courthouse meeting with the District Attorney. This morning he found a note had been slipped under his door from JJ saying that the District Attorney would be the prosecutor on the case and JJ was assisting.

As the waitress brought coffee, he looked at the menu as did Cora and the judge. "I think I'll have eggs benedict," the judge said. "And a glass of orange juice."

Cora put down the menu. "I'm not hungry."

Virgil took her hand. "Trust me, you'll need something on your stomach even if it's just a scrambled egg and toast."

She nodded and when the waitress came they placed their order. Picking up the creamer, the judge spoke up, "I would ask if you've learned anything, but I'd rather hear it in court."

Virgil took a sip of his coffee. "We have a witness holding out. I hope things change."

"Can we call anyone to the stand?"

Virgil looked at Cora. "A few, but not everyone."

They quickly finished breakfast and left for the courthouse. A tall, impressive, limestone building with a double wing, it stood guard over the downtown area of St. Louis.

Inside, the smell of smoke, linseed oil and floor wax filled the air. They walked up the stairs and into the large courtroom with windows facing north. Virgil imagined being in the building brought back a lot of memories for Cora and they weren't good ones. He took her hand and she sat down beside him and tried to smile.

JJ and the District Attorney had their heads together while the two defense lawyers thumbed through stacks of papers. Virgil leaned closer. "It's going to be okay. Just be strong."

"I hate that I have to testify." She grasped his hand. "You'll hear a lot of terrible things about me, but know that I did nothing willingly."

He kissed her cheek. "I know that, sweetheart."

They both turned when Robert and Clare Williams entered the room and sat on the bench across from them. An angry scowl darkened her father's face. Clare, on the other hand, clung to her husband's arm like a dutiful wife.

Judge Steinberg entered from the side door wearing his black robe. He was an impressive man with a full head of gray

142

hair, clean shaven, and intense brown eyes. He slammed down the gavel and the room grew silent.

"We're here to determine if Cora Williams is required to serve thirty more days in prison due to her being released early by mistake."

The taller defense attorney stood up. "Yes sir, that's a ruling, set down by Judge Blackwell. He determined that Miss Williams should serve out her full sentence."

JJ stood. "Miss Williams was given signed released papers. And escorted to the exit of the prison. She had no idea she was being released early. That was a mistake made not by Miss Williams, but the Head Guard, Herbert Grubber. Since her release, Miss Williams has been a model citizen of Gibbs City, Missouri where she has established herself as a doctor in good standing with the community. She is also the sole guardian of her young nephew, Jack Martin. The court would be tearing a family apart and creating a hardship for the young boy."

"This court isn't overly concerned with any hardship Miss Williams might be subjected to."

The portly defense attorney smiled.

"However, I have to ask why we're here? Why go through the expense and time of the trial to put a woman back into a crowded prison for just thirty days?" The judge picked up a piece of paper. "According to the record from the Missouri State Penitentiary for Women, she served four years and eleven months. Isn't that close enough?"

Virgil's heartbeat was so erratic he feared he'd pass out.

The defense attorney stood and straightened his tie. "It's a matter of the right thing being done, your honor. She was sentenced to five years. Not four years and eleven months."

The District Attorney, John Osborn also rose to face the bench. "Since we have been summoned here over this petty matter, your honor, we'd like to prove that sending Miss Williams to jail for accidently shooting Mr. Martin was a gross miscarriage of justice."

The defense council jumped from his seat. "Objection."

Judge Steinberg frowned and glared at Osborn over the rim of his small glasses. "You're talking double jeopardy, Mr. Osborn."

"No, your honor we're not putting Miss Williams back on trial for shooting Dan Martin. She's admitted to that. We're putting Judge Martin and his son on trial for excessive punishment against Miss Williams and the murder of Eleanor Martin."

The room erupted and the judge banged on his desk to regain control. Judge Martin, with his hefty girth, shot to his feet. "I object, your honor. That's an outright lie."

"Gentlemen, in my chamber."

Virgil tightened his grip on Cora's hand.

"What do you think they're up to?" she asked. She leaned toward the judge. "Do they have any evidence that Dan murdered Eleanor? And can they just dismiss everything?"

Virgil stood when Robert Williams stepped over to talk to Cora. "You're still causing trouble. Didn't you learn anything?"

Virgil said, "Other than you're a complete and total monster?"

"You shut up or you'll get that badge ripped right off your chest."

Virgil pressed his body against the older man. "You want to try that?"

Cora shuddered. "Let it go, Virgil."

But he couldn't. "I happen to believe Dan Martin killed Eleanor and I'm not going to stop until I prove it."

Her father growled. "You're getting in way over your head."

Cora took Virgil's arm. "So, you think I should go back to prison? Knowing I'll never walk out."

"That's absurd. Becker gave me his word nothing would happen to you."

"And you believe him? After what he did to me while I was incarcerated?"

Her father turned aside, shaking his head. "Don't be melodramatic. I'm not stupid. I know everything that happened in there."

"Then you're more of a bastard than I thought."

The door to the chamber opened and they all filed out. When the judge was seated, he announced, "I've listened to both sides and this trial will continue. The District Attorney says he has proof of Dan Martin's involvement in the murder of Eleanor Martin and that his father obstructed justice to see that his son didn't go to trial."

Virgil took a deep breath and lowered his head.

"As for Miss Williams, Judge Blackwell's ruling will have no power in this courtroom. If the defense can prove that Dan Martin and Judge Martin are not involved, Miss Williams will return to the Missouri State Penitentiary for Women for thirty days, after which time her debt to society will be fulfilled."

CHAPTER THIRTY

Judge Steinberg's words sent chills down Cora's spine. She had to suppress the urge to stand up and run from the proceedings. How could she ever go back there? And how could her father be so naive. For him to think that a man like Warden Becker could be believed was insane. He obviously knew nothing about the man.

She turned to see Warden Becker sitting right behind her with a sinister leer on his face. "I can hardly wait," he whispered. "It'll be like old times."

"Don't count on it, Becker," Virgil said. "She's not going anywhere."

"We'll see."

"Oh, we're going to see all right. I have a few surprises for you. I hope you told your family goodbye this morning because you're not walking out of here a free man."

Detective David Batcher came in and sat on the end of the row. He looked at Virgil and nodded. Cora wondered what those two had been up to and what had they learned. Did she stand a chance of putting all this behind her?

Poor Jack. Would he live the life she dreamed for him or would this all turn his world upside down? So much uncertainty and fear gnawed at her. Her body felt drawn and tight as a bow. Virgil looked exhausted. She knew he'd been working night and day to find any evidence they could use to help in the situation. She prayed he had, but who could tell at this point? All their lives hung in the balance.

The defense stood and took several papers up to the sidebar. JJ and John Osborn joined them. When they returned to their seats, the judge looked out over the crowd. "Defense has requested a jury, but in this case I'm going to refuse since this wasn't brought to the attention of the court until now."

The chubby defense council stood and held out his arms. "But, your honor, there is a lot at stake here."

"You're here because you want a woman to go back to prison for a month. I'm capable of determining if a case goes to jury or not." He looked over the top of his glass. "Proceed."

"Your honor, we'll prove that all the claims made by the District Attorney and attorney Joseph Johnson are a desperate attempt to obstruct the court's intent to see that Miss Williams serves her full sentence. We question why Miss Williams is determined to fight these proceedings when she was found guilty and ordered to serve her full sentence."

Osborn stood. "Judge Steinberg, this isn't about Miss Williams going back to prison. We're here to determine if there was misconduct involving a judge of the court of Missouri, known to be good friends to Judge Martin. The court questions, was the said judge doing Judge Martin a favor when he convicted a person to five years in prison for a minor offense?"

The judge studied the papers on his desk. "I'm friends with many judges, including Mr. Martin. That doesn't sway my opinion in the least."

"I'll admit that's an admirable statement, but we all know that, in some cases, friendships and favors go a long way."

"I find it hard to believe Judge Blackwell was influenced."

"I can't prove that," Osborn admitted. "But I do know that Judge Blackwell has a gambling problem and is known to borrow large sums of money."

The defense stood up. "Objection. Prosecution has no evidence of that statement. His personal life has nothing to do with this trial."

"Actually, I do." Osborn held out a piece of paper. "Here is a canceled check from Judge Martin to Judge Blackwell in the sum of twenty thousand dollars. The date of the check is the day before Cora Williams was sentenced to five years in prison."

"Objection," the defense shouted. "This evidence wasn't submitted prior to trial."

"It doesn't have to be." The judge ruled, peering over his glasses at the frantic defense attorneys. "The reason we're here is to get to the truth."

"That doesn't prove that Judge Martin bribed anyone."

Judge Steinberg took the evidence and studied it carefully. "Judge Martin, would you stand?"

"I can explain that Jacob. Milford had some medical problems and needed surgery. I simply loaned him the money he needed for his health."

Osborn stood and turned to Martin. "Is that why he spent two weeks in Miami?"

Judge Martin shrugged and smirked. "Perhaps it was part of his recuperation."

Osborn pressed on. "A study of Judge Martin's finances did not show where the money was repaid."

Martin held out his hands. "We made other arrangements."

"Highly suspicious," said Judge Steinberg.

Martin cocked his head. "Still, that's not proof of guilt."

"Your honor," pressing the other lawyer to his seat, the tall defense attorney said, "can we get back to Miss Williams?"

"I'll allow the prosecution to lay out its case."

JJ rose and Cora hoped he could provide something to help her case. Twisting the hankie she'd removed from her purse, she nibbled her bottom lip. The toast she'd had for breakfast sat like a stone in her stomach.

"Your honor, Sheriff Virgil Carter and I went to the Missouri State Penitentiary for Women and we can testify to the horrific conditions there, but first I'd like to lay out some facts."

"Proceed."

"Exhibit A is the original death certificate for Eleanor Martin." He handed it to Judge Steinberg. "Here is the original death certificate. You'll note the first one was signed by a certified Medical Examiner by the name of Timothy Beck. On there he says the cause of death is homicide. A bullet wound to the left side of her temple at a range of about three to four feet."

"I see that. Is Mr. Beck in the courtroom?"

A tall man with long, dark hair, wearing glasses, stood and raised his hand. "I am, your honor."

"Please be seated and if necessary you must be prepared to take the witness stand."

"I understand."

The prosecutor continued. "On the other hand, the death certificate filed with the county is signed by Judge Martin and states that Eleanor Martin committed suicide. Going directly against the determination of the Medical Examiner who'd consulted with an outside source to prove his decision."

"Mr. Beck, who did you use as your second opinion?"

"Doctor Raymond Seymour from New York City. He's one of the most renowned specialists on suicide."

"What did he say? And remember you're under oath."

"He told me that shot was fired from too far away to be suicide. The victim's reach wasn't that long, nor was she left handed. We both concluded Mrs. Martin had been shot at close range, but not close enough to be suicide. When Sheriff Carter and Detective Batcher came to my office, they took the bullet and determined it came from a gun of the same caliber as one owned by the Martins."

"Objection." The defense council shouted. "Where is the proof of this?"

"Did you see the gun?" the judge asked.

"Yes, sir. Detective Batcher presented it to me."

The prosecution turned. "Where did he find this hypothetical gun?"

Beck straightened his glasses. "Oh, the gun wasn't in question. We already knew about it because it was used to prove that Mrs. Martin had committed suicide."

JJ stood. "Did you tell Judge Martin that Eleanor Martin had been murdered?"

Beck nodded. "I did, sir."

"And what did he say?"

"He refused to accept the outcome and wouldn't allow me to submit the correct report."

JJ looked at Judge Steinberg. "Can a judge do that?"

"No." The judge pointed to Martin. "Stand up." He motioned for the bailiff. "Swear him in." Afterwards, Steinberg faced the man. "What do you have to say about this?"

"I knew my son's wife. She was very high-strung, given to fits of depression. I hate to admit, but she was very unhappy. Since I had special knowledge to her state of mind, I knew that she'd killed herself."

"The autopsy proved you wrong, yet you lied as to the cause of her death. Was it to protect your son?"

"No, no, of course not. My son wouldn't hurt a flea. He loved his wife dearly and was devastated at her death."

Cora stood up. "Is that why he was having an affair with Joann Holmes?"

"Quiet," the judge shouted. "No further outbursts."

Cora was so angry she couldn't fight back the tears. Virgil pulled her back down and rested her head on his shoulder.

"Was your son having an affair, Judge Martin?"

"I don't know all the intimate details of my son's life, but I know he loved Eleanor, as we all did."

The judge called over the bailiff and said something Cora couldn't understand.

"Mr. Dan Martin is being summoned to this court. I have to say, I find this all highly unusual. A woman is murdered and no one is held responsible. Then the sister of that person is sentenced to five years in jail for assaulting the man who she obviously suspected killed her sister. I don't even see a medical report on his injury."

The prosecution stood. "All of this is alleged evidence. There is no official report of Mrs. Martin's death except the one filed in the county courthouse."

Judge Steinberg folded his hands and removed his glasses. "Are you saying that due to a judge's actions, far beyond his legal jurisdiction, that ruling should be upheld in a court of law?"

"I'm saying everything else is circumstantial evidence."

"Let me explain something to you, Mr. Stone. In my court, the truth outweighs everything. If Eleanor Martin was murdered, her killer will be found, prosecuted and he'll pay dearly. That's how my court works."

The judge pushed back his chair. "We will adjourn until one, at which time I want Dan Martin in my courtroom and Miss Joann Holmes."

Cora straightened and glanced at her parents. While much of the conversation had been about their deceased daughter, neither showed any signs of distress. Instead they stared straight ahead and exited the courtroom without speaking to anyone.

"You'd think they didn't care their daughter was murdered and that the person responsible was sitting in the same room."

"That's assuming Judge Martin killed Eleanor instead of Dan."

"Regardless of who pulled the trigger, we know that the old man was always in charge."

Judge Garner walked up beside her and took her arm. "I'm grateful Jacob is not settling for what another judge says, but wants the truth to come out."

At the door she leaned heavily on Virgil. "I don't think I can make it through the whole trial. It's too much. I'm already exhausted."

Virgil wrapped his arm around her shoulders and they went down the staircase, outside into the biting wind. Snow swirled lightly in the air, but the coolness against her face felt refreshing.

"We have time to go back to the hotel if you want or we can grab lunch."

The judge pulled his coat closer. "You look like you could use a bed, Virgil. When's the last time you slept?"

"I don't know, but I'm fine. Hopefully I can catch a few winks tonight."

She looked at him. "What are you doing tonight?"

"Batcher and I are still running down leads. We've been what you might call lucky, but we haven't hit pay dirt yet."

"Please must be careful. You're messing with some desperate men. They'll do anything to save their hides. Murder means nothing to them."

Virgil stretched and yawned. "I could go for a sandwich and a cup of coffee. How about you guys?"

Cora nodded. "That sounds nice. There a café right around the corner. Popular place that's known for quick service."

As they crossed the street, Batcher ran up. "I'm out for about an hour. Something came up. You with me, Virgil?"

Virgil let go of her and looked at the judge. "Take care of Cora. We'll be back before court's back in session."

He was gone before she could say goodbye. "It didn't take us long to lose him."

The judge chuckled. "That man's like a dog on a bone. He won't give up until he finds what he's looking for."

"I'm proud he's so brave, but I also worry about him."

The judge took her arm. "I can't tell you not be concerned, because you will be anyway, but I can tell you that he'll never change."

CHAPTER THIRTY-ONE

Virgil and Batcher left the downtown area and drove into the seedier part of town where the FBI agent, Gene McKinnon, stood next to the man from Chicago. They were expected. Virgil and Gene shook hands. "This is David Batcher, St. Louis Detective." After shaking hands they all looked at the man who'd only arrived in town earlier that morning.

He clasped Virgil on the arm. "So, are you going to get me into a witness protection program?"

Virgil knew Dominic Magana from when they served together in Okinawa. He was a hell of a fighter.

"I'll try my best. Judge Steinberg is a fair man. He'll do what's right."

The man lifted his collar and lit a cigarette. He was tall and lean with his black hair slicked back. Wearing a suit and expensive coat, he carried himself like all Italians, brave and brash. "I got what you need but I'm not sure I can testify."

"Whatever you have," Virgil said. "It's no good unless you can swear to everything in court."

"But I gotta lay low until tomorrow. Nothing can happen until I know you held up your end of the bargain."

"We did," Batcher said. "There's no reason for us not to."

"Okay, I'll see you guys later."

Virgil's old Marine buddy hunkered down inside his coat, walked to the corner then disappeared. "You think he'll show?"

"I wouldn't swear to it but what choice do we have? It was him or we had nothing."

Virgil slipped on his gloves. "I'm not too sure we still have anything."

"It went pretty good this morning in court." Batcher tapped him on the shoulder. "Did you know Dan Martin had a girlfriend?"

Virgil shook his head. "That was as much a shock to me as it was to you. But, I never asked Cora much about Dan and she offered very little." They headed for the parked car. "I still don't get how it was so damned easy for Martin to get away with murder while Cora went to prison. I just can't get that in my head."

"Me either and I have a feeling after this trial, there's going to be some changes at City Hall. Those fat bastards are going to be crying for their mommas."

"I sure as hell hope so." Batcher started up the car and they pulled away from the curb.

"Let's find something to eat, I'm cold, tired and hungry."

"Same here. My wife thinks I'm having an affair," Batcher said. "I had to scratch my head at that one. Where the hell did she expect I'd get the energy for that?"

"That's the life of law enforcement."

They headed downtown. "You going to ask Cora to marry you?"

"I already have, but she's stalling. After five years in that hellhole she's scared to death of men and I don't blame her. That's the reason she's not going back."

"But you know in your heart that's a possibility, right?"

"I can't let that happen."

"Would you honestly break the law?"

"Do you think the true law had anything to do with her being put in prison?"

"No, she was set up, that's for sure."

"So, why would I respect and uphold a law like that?"

Batcher slapped him on the back. "Because that's the kind of man you are. Someone has to be the good guy."

After stopping at a local diner, they grabbed a quick sandwich and a cup of coffee. Just as they started up the courthouse steps, Dan Martin and his father blocked their path. "I hope you know what you're getting into, Sheriff Carter."

"Oh, I think I do."

"And you, Detective David Batcher, I've already got you fired."

"I haven't heard that, but then since I'm working for the Attorney General right now, my boss may not know that he can't fire me."

"It won't be long," the elder Martin sneered.

They all entered the building and entered the courtroom. Virgil moved across to sit next to Cora. "Did you eat lunch?"

"I should be asking you that. The way you and Mr. Batcher took off I wasn't sure you'd make it back in time, much less eat."

"I'm fine." He smiled and put his arm around her. "I'm just fine."

The judge came in and they all stood until he was seated then the District Attorney called Dan Martin to the stand.

He asked Dan a lot of questions Virgil already knew the answer to, but it got interesting when Miss Joann Holmes was mentioned. Dan lowered his head and dabbed at his dry eyes. "I was unfaithful to my wife. It was just a silly fling and something I'll always regret."

Osborn had turned into a bulldog. "You say it was a silly fling?"

"Yes sir."

"Then why do you continue to see Miss Holmes? As early as last Saturday night?"

"That was just a friendly drink."

"At the Carlton Hotel, where you both spent the night?"

"Objection, your honor," defense called. "A man having an affair doesn't make him a murderer. If it did, half the men in the county would be in jail."

Mr. Stone might have chuckled, but no one else did, including the judge. "That may be the case with some, Mr. Stone, but in this particular situation it can also be motive to murder your wife."

"I didn't murder her, judge. She killed herself."

The DA put his hands behind his back and approached the witness. "Tell us what led up to that night."

"We'd been out to dinner and," Dan wiped his brow and looked at his father as if hoping for guidance. "She was real sad about something."

"You didn't know what she was upset about?"

"No, I just know she was. Then she took the gun out of my father's desk and shot herself."

"So, you were in your father's office?"

"Yes."

"What were you doing there?"

Dan looked like a ten year old in the principal's office. "What do you mean?"

"I mean, was it common when your wife was so upset that you would be in your father's office. Not in the upstairs living room or your bedroom?"

Dan wiped his face again and looked helplessly at his father. "Usually we have drinks down there with my parents."

"But, you stated to the police officers that you were alone in the room together."

"We were."

"Were you fighting, Mr. Martin? Did you maybe have a quarrel over something?" The man paused. "Perhaps over Miss Holmes?"

"No, we weren't mad at each other and she didn't know anything about Joann."

John Osborn put his hands in his pockets and pinned a hard stare on the nervous man on the stand. "Mr. Martin, you expect the court to believe that your wife was so distraught that while the two of you were in your father's office, not arguing, no loud voices, and no crying, Eleanor Martin pulled a gun out of a desk drawer and shot herself in the head before you could stop her?"

"That's what happened."

The District Attorney flashed him a skeptical look then sat down.

Dan pounded the pulpit in front of him. "That's what happened."

The rotund defense attorney stood. "Mr. Martin did you kill your wife?"

"No." He lowered his head and laced his fingers together. "I did not."

"Did you even have a reason to kill her?"

"No."

"Was she insured for a lot of money?"

Martin looked surprised at the question. "No."

"So you gained nothing from the death of your wife?"

"Only heartache." This time, Dan Martin cried real tears.

CHAPTER THIRTY-TWO

Cora felt as cold as a marble statue. Her parents appeared so untouched and oblivious to the death of their own daughter that her mother didn't once bring a hankie to her eyes.

While the conversation in the courtroom circled around Eleanor's death, no one could know her grief. Of the separation, the despair and the knowledge that a wonderful young mother, with an infectious smile no longer existed except in her heart.

Joann's time on the witness stand was brief and damning to Dan. Apparently they'd had an ongoing relationship for over six years. Certainly not the light fling Dan had described.

The District Attorney called Mr. Batcher's Captain, Gerald Tate, to the stand. He was a big man who was used to throwing his massive weight around. His thinning hair, droopy mustache and thick lips, along with constant eye movement, made him appear shady and suspicious.

"Captain Tate, did you see the original death certificate for Eleanor Martin?"

Confident and arrogant, Captain Tate leaned back and hitched up his trousers. "Not that I recall."

Osborn pushed harder. "Do you recall the incident at all?"

"I remember sending a couple of detectives out to arrest Miss Cora Williams."

"Where did that order come from?"

"Judge Martin. He said Miss Williams had broken into their home and shot his son in the leg."

"Was Mr. Martin taken to the hospital or seen by a doctor?"

"Not that I'm aware of."

"So what charges were filed against her?"

"Assault and attempted murder."

"But you said she broke into the house."

"Dan, I mean, Mr. Martin later admitted he opened the door and allowed Miss Williams to enter."

"The day *after* the incident she was charged with attempted murder? And only on the say so of Judge Martin."

"Objection, your honor," the defense shouted. "Is Miss Williams back on trial for murder? Weren't we reminded that would be double jeopardy?"

"What's on trial is whether the charges filed against Miss Williams were justified and fair according to the law." Judge Steinberg looked at John Osborn. "Continue."

"So, you charged her with attempted murder. Why?"

"She went at him with a gun."

"But she shot him in the leg at a range close enough to have easily blown his head off."

"Can't say, I wasn't there."

"But, you had no problem with arresting her for attempted murder after speaking to Judge Martin." The District Attorney paced. "I mean, you're a pretty smart guy. You didn't get to the top of the St. Louis police department without knowing the score. Am I correct, Captain?"

Tate squirmed. "Yeah, I suppose so."

"Yet, you sent two detectives out in the middle of the night to arrest a prominent doctor for attempted murder without knowing anything about the case. Not even a medical report that he'd been shot."

"Yeah, that's my job."

The District Attorney held up a piece of paper. "This is an affidavit from the two investigating detectives, Alder White and Boyd Calhoun. In this signed testimonial, they state that they wrote out a report of the incident and cited it as a domestic disturbance."

"I took another look and changed the charges. I'm the Captain. I have the right to do that."

"Even when the two investigating detectives didn't agree and went so far as to refuse to sign the report you shoved in front of them?"

"It's not up to them." He thumped his chest. "I make those decisions."

"And, of course, you weren't persuaded in any way by Judge Martin?"

"No."

"After Miss Williams' arrest you were seen having dinner in a popular restaurant with Judge Martin and his son, Dan."

"So, I'm allowed to eat anywhere I want and with who I want."

"You're right, Captain Tate, but I hold in my hands a copy of your bank transactions from five years ago and the day after Miss Williams was sent to jail, five thousand dollars was deposited in your account." The DA looked at the people in the courtroom. "And at the same time, that exact same amount of money was withdrawn from Judge Martin's personal account."

Gasps filled the room.

When John sat down at the table with JJ, the defense attorneys huddled together, before one of them stood to question the captain. "How many commendations have you been given in your twenty years of exemplary service with the police department, Captain Tate?"

Tate grinned. "Sixteen distinguished merit badges, two medals for bravery in the line of duty and two outstanding achievement awards."

The lawyer sat down with a smug look on his face.

"Cross examine, your honor?" John asked.

The judge nodded.

"The records state that all but two of those commendations were issued by one Judge Martin." John folded his hands behind him. "Is that correct?"

"I earned every one of those."

"According to Judge Martin." He turned away. "No further questions."

"I'd like to call Miss Cora Williams to the stand."

She stood on legs as weak as a newborn's and as wobbly as a spinning top. Virgil patted her gently on the back and winked. "Now's your chance, baby."

She tried to smile but failed. The distance between her seat and the witness box seemed miles. She managed to get seated and held up her hand to take the oath.

John Osborn approached her with a smile. "Miss Williams, I truly believe you were unlawfully charged and forced to serve time for a crime you did not commit."

"Objection," called an attorney from the defense table.

"Overruled," the judge said. "But watch yourself, counselor."

"Did you go to Dan Martin's house with the intent to kill him on the night in question?"

"Yes, I did."

"But you didn't. Was it lack of opportunity?"

"Objection, putting words in the witness's mouth."

"I'll accept that."

"No, but I was still furious. Dan started crying and swore he didn't kill Eleanor. That he loved her."

"Did that change your mind?"

"No, it was the thought of my nephew, Jack, losing both parents that preyed on my mind."

"So, instead of murdering him in cold blood, you nicked him in the leg."

"Objection, the exact extent of the injury hasn't been proven."

Osborn continued. "As a doctor you would know if he required stitches. Did he?"

"No."

John turned to the people in the room. "So tell the court what happened when you, not someone else, but you, called the police."

"They arrived. By then I'd applied a bandage and Dan was sipping a glass of whiskey."

"Why didn't you run?"

"I felt I should face up to what I'd done. I shot a man and felt the law wouldn't look kindly on that."

"Was there anyone else in the house?"

"Not that I'm aware of."

"When Officers White and Calhoun came, what happened?"

"I explained what happened. I gave them the gun and they put me in the police car and took me downtown."

"Did they handcuff you?"

"No, sir."

"Did they question you at the station?"

"Yes, they were very polite. I told them I thought Dan Martin had murdered my sister and I was upset and wanted him to pay, but I couldn't bring myself to kill a man."

"Did they lock you up?"

"No, they had a patrolman take me home."

"So, they freed a person who was later convicted of attempted murder?"

"They didn't say anything about charges. They did tell me to stay away from the Martins and to take a few days to mourn my sister."

"What happened the next night?"

"The same two officers came to my home, handcuffed me and took me to the station where I was put in a cell for twenty-four hours."

"During that time did you call an attorney?"

"I wasn't even allowed to go to the bathroom. They just ignored me."

"What happened next?"

"My father came to the jail, said he'd hired an attorney and they were waiting for a trial date."

"You weren't released?"

"No, I didn't know that was an option."

"So you waited in the police jail for how long?"

"After my father left, they moved me to another part of the building where I had a cell with a toilet, but I never got to leave it until my trial twelve days later."

"So, you sat in jail for thirteen days. Who came to see you?"

"No one. Just the guard who brought me my food."

Visibly angered, John said, "So no visitors, no exercise, limited human contact and no access to your attorney."

"That's correct."

Judge Steinberg looked at her. "Miss Williams, did you ever see the arresting officers again?"

"No."

"You saw no one except the guard who fed you. Is that correct?"

"Yes, sir."

The chubby defense attorney bounced up.

"Sit down, Mr. Fisher," the judge said sternly. "You may take your seat, Miss Williams." The judge pointed his gavel. "Captain Tate I'm recalling you to the stand."

"I object, your honor," the taller attorney said. "Captain Tate has already testified."

"Sit down, Mr. Stone. I won't tell you again."

Captain Gerald Tate didn't seem so cocky this time. The judge reminded him he was still under oath and ordered the attorney to continue.

"Did you knowingly leave a young woman in your jail for thirteen days without proper facilities, without letting her outside for air, and without visitation from her representative?"

Tate fidgeted uncomfortably in the chair. "I didn't think it'd take that long."

"Who suggested that Miss Williams not be given bail nor advised of her legal rights?" The judge pointed to him with a warning glare. "Be very careful how you answer because your retirement, your career and our reputation are at stake here."

Loosening his collar, Tate swallowed several times. "I did what Judge Martin and her father told me to do."

Shocked gasps filled the room. Cora leaned forward and looked down at her father who sat as tall and straight as a righteous man.

The judge slammed the gavel down so hard it echoed loudly throughout the room. "This court finds that Miss Cora Williams was unlawfully charged with a crime she did not commit, she was the victim of a gross misjustice and collusion. Her sentence is revoked." He wasn't through. Glaring at Captain Tate he said, "Captain Tate, you are stripped of all your duties, medals and pension. You will immediately surrender your badge and weapon to the bailiff and you are immediately relieved of duty."

Judge Steinberg smacked the gavel again. "We'll convene again tomorrow morning at eight."

The defense attorney, Mr. Stone, stood. "For what, your honor? Miss Williams has been exonerated."

"Tomorrow we reopen the murder case of Mrs. Eleanor Martin and alleged corruption in the investigation." The judge stood. "Anyone not present in my courtroom at eight in the morning will be arrested by the FBI and dragged into this court and charged with contempt."

Cora cried out in relief and collapsed weakly into Virgil's arms.

CHAPTER THIRTY-THREE

Virgil was so glad to get out of the stuffy courtroom and into the fresh air he practically ran to the exit. He escorted Cora to the judge then rushed out to talk to Batcher. "Make sure you hold on to our friend from Chicago."

"McKinnon has him in a local hotel. He's not letting him out of his sight."

"Good, if there isn't anything else, I think I'm going to grab some sleep tonight." Virgil rubbed his hand over his face. "I'm exhausted."

"I know how you feel. It's hell fighting crime. Especially when you don't know who to trust."

"Yes, it is." Virgil looked at Cora waiting by the exit with the judge. "They really put her through hell."

"I can't tell you how happy I was when Judge Steinberg stuck it to Tate. I knew he was crooked from the first day I met him. And now we know who's been having us followed."

"But I don't think he had anything to do with the road block."

"Maybe not directly, but how did they know where we were?"

"Good point. I'm beat, see you in the morning."

Virgil met up with Cora and the judge. He reached out, took her hand and brought her fingers to his lips. "Let's go." Following the judge, they started down the granite steps.

Cora's father waited there, his face hard and stern. "You're quite a disappointment, young lady. You've caused more trouble than you can ever imagine."

"Really, you have the nerve to walk up and speak to me after all the things you allowed them to do to me?"

He flung back his hand to slap her, but Virgil grabbed his arm and twisted. "Don't lay a hand on her. Don't you dare touch her."

He released Williams with a shove and they left for the hotel. With his arm around her, he felt her body shake with anger.

"He's so vile. I swear, I don't understand the man. What did I ever do to deserve his hatred?"

"He can't touch you now. So, let's go to the hotel, get rested up, have dinner and call Jack."

The judge hailed a cab. "That sounds like a perfect way to celebrate."

Virgil followed Cora into her room at the hotel. She removed her coat, kicked off her shoes and fell back on the bed, her arms spread out wide. "I can't tell you how tired I am."

"You don't know the half of it."

"I can imagine. You and Detective Batcher have uncovered so much that not even I knew. You've been quite busy."

"There is much more to come. Be prepared for anything because once the DA opens the case against Judge Martin and your father, all restrictions will be removed and we can see how big this case really gets."

"You mean it wasn't just about placing the blame on me so Dan wouldn't go to jail?"

"I doubt that was even figured in."

"How horrible," she sighed as she got up. Hugging herself, she paced the floor. "I can't imagine what makes these men so dishonest and callous. They have no compassion in them at all."

"They're men of corruption and greed is all they know." He stepped over and wrapped her in his arms just to hold her still and keep her from getting more agitated. "This will be over soon and we'll go back to our normal lives."

"Ha, normal."

"Yeah, where I'm always asking you to marry me and you always saying no."

She looked into his eyes and their lips met. The need for her grew inside him like a storm. Making love to her was all he thought about day and night. He wanted to claim her as his own again and again.

She gently broke the kiss then traced her finger along his bottom lip. If she knew what that did you him, she'd quit. "It won't be no forever. Hopefully this trial will put things to rest."

"You know you still have to testify about your time in prison. John Osborn isn't going to pass on that. He's determined to make some major changes at the prison and put Warden Becker behind bars permanently."

"I'd love to see that. He belongs in a cage."

A knock sounded at the door and Virgil opened it greeting JJ with a smile. "How are we doing?" Virgil asked.

"Better than I thought. I wasn't sure Judge Steinberg was going to allow the evidence against Captain Tate. I'm glad he did." JJ touched her face. "They should've never treated you like that."

"The disturbing thing is, my father could've prevented it all. His high powered attorneys had the clout and prestige to get me out on bail and the charges reduced to a misdemeanor. I can't stop wondering what Judge Martin has over my father that would make him desert me like that."

JJ sat down. "I don't know if that's the case. It very well could be, but maybe your father has a personal vendetta against you."

"But why?"

"I searched, Cora. I tried to find anything I could to justify your father's conduct toward you, but there isn't anything I could come up with. I'd even considered you might not be his legitimate child, but you are."

"I never thought of that."

JJ smiled softly. "Well, don't. Your mother was and always has been a perfectly proper lady."

"Really?"

"I contacted several people in her hometown and she was a very respected lady with a flawless reputation. And, you were born one year and six months after the marriage. So, nothing there."

Rubbing her forehead, she looked out the window. "That's a relief, I guess. I almost wish I weren't his child. At least then I wouldn't have his blood running through my veins."

Virgil walked over and hugged her. "We can't choose our families."

JJ stood. "I just dropped by to let you know I'll be tied up the rest of the night, probably until the wee hours of the morning. John learned there's a witness from out of town that wants to talk. FBI Agent McKinnon has him holed up in a local hotel."

"Good luck," Cora called. She smiled up at Virgil. "Can we call Jack? I miss him so much and he has to be so worried."

"Sure, he's home from school by now."

Cora dialed Maggie's number and when Brigs answered, she asked for Jack. The sound of his little voice sent a wave of warmth all over her body. She loved him with all her heart. "Hi Jack, how was school?"

"Aunt Cora, are you coming home soon?"

"I hope so." She looked at Virgil and smiled. "I miss you so much."

"I miss you too, but I get to stay with Tommy and we have lots of fun." Tommy yelled a greeting in the background. "Is Uncle Virgil there?"

"Yes, he is. Do you want to say hello?"

"Yes, please."

She handed the phone to Virgil who immediately started laughing and teasing Jack. She heard the young boy's giggles from across the room. "And guess what," Virgil said. "I bought you a present."

There was a pause. "No, I'm not telling you. It's a surprise."

Silence again. "No, Aunt Cora can't tell you because she doesn't know. You're going to have to wait. Okay, be a good boy and we'll see you soon. Put Aunt Maggie on the phone for Aunt Cora."

Cora took the phone and Maggie asked, "How's everything in St. Louis?"

"Nerve-wracking and uncomfortable. The judge did throw out the order for me to return to prison. So, I don't have that to worry about. I've been exonerated."

"That's wonderful. Anything else is just gravy on the potatoes."

"You're right. My parents are here and it's so painful. My mother hasn't even looked at me and when we left the courthouse my father tried to slap me."

"That's terrible, Cora, and I feel awful for you. But Gibbs City is your home and we all love and care about you. Leave all that anger and hurt in St. Louis where it belongs."

"I will and thank you, Maggie, for being such a good friend."

She hung up and turned to Virgil who lay on the bed half asleep. When she walked by he reached out and took her hand.

"I could use a little nap before dinner." He smiled and pulled her closer. "Maybe a little something else."

"It's still light outside."

"So, pull the curtains and come to bed."

CHAPTER THIRTY-FOUR

Cora woke wrapped tightly in Virgil's arms. She turned and buried her nose in his neck, inhaling his masculine scent. She snuggled closer and he groaned as she nibbled his left ear. "While this feels wonderful," he said. "I'm starving."

They dressed quickly and made their way to the sidewalk. The evening air was biting cold and made Cora want to get something hot and go back to the room. She blew into her hands as Virgil opened the door of the small cafe. She giggled like a school girl when his lips swept across her mouth.

The cozy diner was very nice and Cora decided she needed a glass of wine. Virgil had a beer. "It's been awhile since we've been able to sit down across from each other and talk," he said. "I feel like I haven't seen you in a week."

"It feels like that to me as well. I think we'll both be glad when this is over and done with. Really, now that I know I don't have to go back to prison, I can't understand why they won't let me return home."

"The judge might have more questions."

She didn't want to be asked any questions and she certainly didn't want to give up any more than she had to. Virgil had already learned too much. While Becker couldn't hurt her anymore, she still had her pride. She wanted to hold on to it as long as possible.

Maybe someday she'd be honest and tell Virgil everything, but she seriously doubted it. Not the way she loved him. If he knew the whole truth, he'd walk out of her life and never look back. She couldn't stand that. Was it too much to ask to just be happy for once in her life?

"We'll see, but they've already decided to make changes to the prison and put the warden away."

"That may not be over yet. Let's sit back and see how this all turns out."

"I hate being away from Jack."

"I know, but he sounds like he's having fun. You know he loves being around all Maggie's boys."

"I know," She covered his hand. "I just miss our normal routine. Coffee at the kitchen table late at night, Jack sleeping safely in his bed and Earl mooching a piece of pie."

"I miss all that, too. And trust me when I say this will be over very soon and it'll all be nothing but a distant memory."

"I hope so. Every time the judge calls someone up to testify, I get so nervous and frightened."

"Everyone is tense in court. It's normal."

She rested her chin on the palm of her hand. "So, what did you buy Jack?"

He shook his head. "I can't tell you."

"You can't tell me because you haven't bought anything yet."

"Maybe, but regardless, you aren't going to know until he does."

"Please don't let it be another noisy cap gun. Cops and robbers or cowboys and Indians are all those two boys want to play lately."

Virgil laughed. "Let them enjoy their childhood. It doesn't last that long."

They finished eating and he helped her with her coat. Sleeting rain pelted them as they stepped out of the restaurant. They both backed under the awning over the door. "This is miserable", she said.

"It probably won't get any better, so let's make a run for the hotel."

When the traffic cleared, they stepped off the curb. Cora turned as a car drove at them. Virgil grabbed her, spun around and protected her with his body. Four shots thundered in the dark.

A strange and unfamiliar scream ripped through the night air as Virgil slumped to the ground.

Stunned and shaking, Cora bent over Virgil's prone body, trying to shield him from the sleet. "Someone call an ambulance immediately."

She turned him over and lifted his head to her lap. Eyes closed, his skin had already started to whiten. Leaning forward she noticed he was barely breathing. "Someone get help," Cora screamed. A lady stood nearby, a look of horror on her face. "I need you to call an ambulance, this man is dying."

Surprisingly the woman flew into action, knocking over a table and several people in the process. She ran to the bar and picked up the phone. Cora heard the woman's stern voice.

Several people drew closer. "Is he okay?" Who shot him?" What's his name?"

The questions were too many for Cora to process. She struggled to get Virgil's coat unbuttoned and removed. Two elderly gentlemen helped her. She rolled him on his stomach and saw where two of the bullets had hit him. One directly in the center of his back, another closer to his shoulder.

The one in the middle worried her the most. It could very well be deadly. She didn't hear the sirens as the ambulance neared, but the minute the attendants arrived she knew it was best to get out of their way.

As they took out a gurney and slid him into the ambulance, Cora demanded to ride with them. She had to be there. "I'm his friend and I'm a doctor."

She helped them cut off his shirt and examine the wound. The bullet to the shoulder had gone straight through, the other was still somewhere in his body. Blood poured from both wounds, however the one in his shoulder had slowed when a compress was applied.

They arrived at the hospital and Cora jumped out and ran into the hospital. Thank God. "Sam, Doctor Sam Slater."

He turned and looked at her. It took a few minutes for him to recognize her. "Cora, how are you?"

She pointed to the gurney being brought into the hospital. "My dear friend has been shot. Can you please help him?"

"Take him to exam room five, I'm right behind you." He took Cora's arm. "Have a seat. You know I'll do everything I can. He's in good hands."

"Thank you, Sam."

The emergency room was busy and several people stared at her and her blood soaked clothes as she slumped into a nearby hard, wooden chair clutching the remnants of Virgil's shirt. God, it all happened so quickly Cora wondered how they'd gotten here so fast.

After a few minutes, a nurse came over with a cup of water. She had a tablet in her hand. "Do you know the person you came in with?"

"Yes, his name is Sheriff Virgil Carter."

"Is there someone we can call for you?"

A normal person would say her family, instead Cora said, "Please call the Bellaire Hotel, ask for Judge Francis Garner and let him know what's happened."

The nurse walked away and Cora sat holding the cup of water, her heart too heavy for her to take a deep breath. Before long, Sam rushed toward her. She dropped the cup and grabbed Sam's hands. "Is he alive?"

"He is, but he's badly injured and I can't promise anything. I'm taking him to surgery now. Go up to the waiting room and I'll come out as soon as I'm finished."

Sam left but Cora couldn't move. Her arms were limp and she felt stuck in two feet of thick mud. What if he didn't make it? How would she explain it to Jack, Virgil's family, his friends? How does one tell a person's loved ones that they died protecting you?

How could she go on without him?

The nurse took her hand and gently led her up upstairs to the second floor where she sat her in a comfortable chair after removing her blood soaked coat. As Cora huddled in the nondescript room with its beige walls, brown floor and lines of hard chairs, she thought of how often she had been in surgery thinking of those loved ones waiting for news of the patient. How often the news wasn't good, the wonderful times when it was.

Now, she sat on the other side and little did she realize all this time those waiting were hurting much more than the patients she operated on. It was a different pain, but one much more piecing and agonizing than any scalpel could do.

The door opened and she jumped up hoping it was Sam, since she was the only person waiting. But Judge Garner walked in followed by Detective Batcher.

The judge wrapped her in his kind embrace. "How is he, dear?"

"I don't know yet." She sat because she wasn't sure she could stand. "They have him in surgery. I know the doctor. He's one of the best."

Batcher sat next to her. "What happened?"

"We were walking out of the restaurant. We'd finished dinner, had a cup of coffee and were talking about how we missed home and my nephew."

"No one in the restaurant seemed to be watching you?"

She shrugged. "Not that I noticed. Virgil was checking out our surroundings, but that's second nature for him. So, I thought nothing of it."

The judge took her hand. "We heard he was shot. How did that happen?"

"We went to leave. It was sleeting so we stood under the awning a few minutes, then Virgil decided we'd make a run for it. Before we reached the curb I noticed a car coming toward us and it was strange. I didn't know why at the time, but now I remember it was driving down the wrong side of the street."

She slumped back, her head resting on the wall behind her. "Then I heard four shots before the car squealed away."

"How badly was Virgil hit?" the judge asked.

"Twice. Once in the shoulder. That bullet went through and came out the front, but the second bullet hit him square in the back. It could've done too much damage to be repaired. The aorta artery is exactly where he was shot."

Batcher stood and began to pace. "I can't believe they'd try something right in the middle of the trial. And Virgil isn't even on the witness list."

The judge removed his coat. "But he was investigating everything."

"So am I. Why not take a shot at me?" Then Batcher stopped. "Because I'm staying with my sister while my wife and children are out of town. They couldn't find me."

"What?" Cora asked. "I don't understand."

"They might've been gunning for both of us, but I'm at my sister's across town. My mother-in-law became sick, so last night my wife bundled up the kids and drove to Kansas City to stay with her for a few days."

The judge sat down. "They could still try."

Batcher excused himself and stepped outside the glassed in room and picked up the phone. He made several calls before returning to the room. "My wife and kids are fine. I told them to stay put. My neighbor said there's a car parked across the street from my house and it's been there for the last four hours."

"It could be them."

"I've got five squad cars on the way there. I told the officer in charge I want those men alive."

"This just gets worse. I never thought Virgil would get hurt. I didn't want anyone hurt. I regret the day I ever moved to Gibbs City." Tears streamed down her face. "If I lose Virgil, I don't know what I'll do."

The judge put his arm around her. "Let's just pray he makes it through this. He's pretty tough."

"I know, but a bullet like he took can do a lot of damage."

After what seemed like hours, Sam came through the swinging doors. He knelt in front of her and took her hands. Cora had seen that look too many times, had perfected it in her practice, it was the, "I'm sorry" look.

Pain bent her over. A pain unlike she'd never known even in her years of prison, sliced through her like a dull knife. Darkness closed in on her, her fingers and hands went numb and she forgot to breathe. Her heart shattered, splintered and turned to dust in a hollow and empty chest.

CHAPTER THIRTY-FIVE

Cora sat at Virgil's bedside gripping his limp hand in hers. Nothing had changed in the last two days. Sam had said it would be touch and go for several days and the prognosis wasn't good, but she believed he'd survive. She had to. It was that or she'd fall apart at the seams.

The judge had just left with Batcher. They found the men responsible for shooting Virgil and they were secured behind bars. Batcher had been interrogating them ruthlessly.

After learning what happened, Judge Steinberg had postponed court for three days. Tomorrow she'd have to leave Virgil's side and return to the hearings.

Looking at his pale face, Cora fought back tears. She'd already wept enough to drown the poor man. She'd accepted enough blame to wallow in for a lifetime and she'd prayed so hard she feared God was going deaf.

His scratchy beard and cracked lips made her heart hurt. She'd never wanted anything as badly as she wanted Virgil to open his eyes and start talking. He had groaned a few times in the last two days, even mumbled what sounded like her name, but little else.

The nurse brought her a cup of coffee and Cora nodded her thanks then set it on the nightstand. She hadn't been able to hold anything on her stomach while in the hospital and the scent of astringent and medicine made her head pound.

She rolled her stiff shoulders and got up to stand by the window. It looked out over the busy city. Snow fell last night, but the sun came out and melted it all away. Now it left behind brown slush and unhappy drivers.

"Cora."

She turned to the sound of Virgil's rough voice. Darting to the bed, she fell into the chair beside him. "Virgil, are you all right? Are you in any pain?"

He rolled his head to where he could see her and smiled faintly. "Hello, beautiful."

She captured his hand and pressed it against her cheek, fight back tears. "I thought I'd lost you."

"I'm too tough to die."

"Oh, my God." She touched his face, unable to believe he was finally conscious. "Do you remember being shot?"

He slowly brought his hand to rub the center of his chest. "I think so."

"As we left the restaurant, someone fired four bullets at us. You were hit twice. Once in the shoulder, the other in the middle of your back. It nicked your aorta, ruptured your spleen and collapsed your lung. You were in surgery twice to stop the bleeding and repair the damage."

He rubbed his hand over his face and tried to lift his head. "Where are we with the trial?"

"It reconvenes tomorrow."

He tried to sit up. "Can I get out of here by then?"

Putting her hands on his shoulders, she pressed him back onto the bed. "No, you're still in critical condition. You can't go anywhere."

"What about Batcher? Is he okay?"

"Yes, luckily he was at his sister's house. However there were men waiting outside his house."

"Son of a bitch." He tightened his lips. "Did they catch the guys?"

"Yes, with Agent McKinnon's help."

"I hope they spend the rest of their lives behind bars."

"The big question is who sent them to assassinate you and David?"

"They haven't confessed yet?"

"Not that I'm aware of, but the FBI is taking this very seriously."

"You'll be at the trial tomorrow. Stay close to the judge, Batcher and McKinnon. They'll protect you. We don't know for certain one of those bullets wasn't meant for you."

She glanced at the guard sitting outside the door. "I think they've already thought of that."

He took her hand and pulled her closer, brushing his lips against hers. "I don't want to lose you, either."

He grinned. "Are you any closer to saying yes to my proposal?"

"You're relentless."

"I still worry about the possibility you might be carrying my child."

"That's not possible."

"Cora, only God can know that."

"If that's the case, God knows I can't have children. Not ever."

Virgil's grip on her hand loosened and his eyes fluttered before he fell back into a deep sleep. She could hardly wait for the doctor to make his rounds. She had to know if he was getting better or if there was still a chance he could die without notice.

She wiped her tear-filled eyes and adjusted the sheet folded across his chest. He looked better, but as a doctor she knew that could, at times, be deceiving. Also, it wasn't uncommon for a critically ill person to be very lucid before passing away. She prayed that wasn't the case with Virgil.

The nurse came in carrying a small metal tray with a sandwich, an apple and a cup of coffee. "I walked by and heard Mr. Carter speaking. I thought you might feel better and be able to eat something. You have to keep your strength up, too."

The food held no appeal, but Cora forced a smile. "Please set it over there. I think you're right. I do feel well enough to try to eat something."

The nurse checked Virgil's pulse, listened to his chest and lifted an eyelid to check his pupils.

On her way out of the room she stopped and turned to Cora. "Your father was downstairs again today demanding to see you."

Alarm shot through her body and she felt her insides recoil. "I don't want to see him."

"Agent McKinnon has sealed off this area and he and his men aren't letting anyone up but Judge Garner and Detective Batcher."

"Good, please keep it that way."

An hour later Batcher came in and was delighted to hear that Virgil was awake and able to speak. "That's great news. Maybe they'll let him out of here soon."

"Not soon enough," Virgil murmured. "I want out now."

Batcher moved closer. "You're taking it easy, buddy. They almost killed you. It's important you heal up."

"Trial?"

"I'm staying close to Cora, she won't be out of my sight." He looked at her. "Virgil, I want you to tell her to go to the hotel and get some rest tonight. She's been at your side for days. I'll have two men right outside her door."

While she shook her head, Virgil looked at her. "Get some sleep tonight, honey. You'll need it for court tomorrow. Batcher will take good care of you. I'd trust him with my life, I trust him with yours."

"But I want to be with you."

Dr. Slater came in and stood in the middle of the room. He held up his finger. "No arguing with the patient."

Cora looked up. "But," she stammered, afraid they'd kick her out and she wouldn't be here if he needed her. "I want to be with him."

Sam put his arm around her. "He's made a turn. By the looks of him, he's going to make it. What he needs now is rest." He held her in front of him. "You're exhausted, young lady. I want you to get some food in your stomach and a good night's sleep in a real bed tonight."

She tried to object, but Sam shook his finger at her. "Doctor's orders."

Not happy with Sam's ultimatum, Cora left after much arguing. She agreed to let Batcher take her back to the hotel room and place a guard outside her room. Leaving Virgil had been the most difficult thing she'd ever done.

At her hotel room, David went inside first to check every nook and cranny. Satisfied, he said, "Stay in your room. Have your meals brought up here, and I'll pick you and the judge up at seven thirty tomorrow. That should give us plenty of time to get to the courthouse."

With her hand on the door, she smiled. "Thank you, David, for being such a good friend to Virgil. I appreciate all you've done for us."

"Just stay in the room."

"I promise."

"Good."

He left and Cora bolted the door. Suddenly the last few days caught up with her and she slumped into a nearby chair. She'd never thought life could get this complicated or difficult. Resting her head on the back of the cushioned chair she let out a breath and relived the moment Virgil had been shot.

The familiar feelings rushed back. She thought he was dead. Even later there was little evidence he'd pull through. When rushed into surgery for the second time, Cora felt her time had run out. But again, Virgil surprised her. He'd lived despite the odds.

Anger simmered in her heart and an overwhelming desire rushed through her to go to the jail and tell those who tried to kill him what lowly cowards they were. To try to kill an honorable man who'd served his country, suffered the pain of losing two brothers and cared so deeply for those under his responsibility.

What kind of men did awful things like that? Why were they even born?

Bitterness brought her to her feet and had her pacing the room. This whole situation had been her fault. She was the one who'd had to make Dan Martin pay. She was the one who felt so damned invincible that she allowed an irrational action to take over common sense.

Those who'd done this would pay. She didn't care who found out what. She was going to bury the three men who she felt pulled the trigger and tried to murder the man she loved.

No more secrets.

CHAPTER THIRTY-SIX

The next morning, arriving at the courthouse, David had Cora and the judge completely surrounded by armed men. As she started up the stairs she saw her father. He waited at the top, his coat draped over his arm, his hat in his hand.

"Cora, I'd like to speak to you," he demanded. Not requested, but insisted.

She glared at him. "No you don't because you're not going to like what comes out of my mouth."

Entering the courtroom, Cora refused to sit on the same side of the room as her parents. She wanted to be as far from them as possible.

The judge entered and they all rose then took their seats. Judge Steinberg looked out among the people in the courtroom. "It has come to my attention that Sheriff Virgil Carter was shot outside a local downtown restaurant and remains in serious condition. The perpetrators were caught and FBI Agent Gene McKinnon has gotten a confession and is in the process of checking out that information. I'm assured arrest warrants are forthcoming."

Murmurs buzzed across the room. The District Attorney stood. "Those men were also paid to take out Detective David Batcher. He's convinced the trail of evidence will lead back to Judge Albert Martin. At this time, the State requests that Mr. Martin be placed under arrest."

Judge Steinberg slammed down his gavel and said, "Put the handcuffs on him. You're under arrest for hiring three men to commit murder."

"That's absurd," Judge Martin shouted. "You can't prove anything."

"Don't count on that," John said. "Gene McKinnon has a reputation of getting to the truth of the matter. I have all the confidence in the world that he'll be reporting to this court before the end of the day."

The defense attorney stood. "Your honor I request that Warden Becker be released on his own recognizance until his trial."

"I have just reached my decision on Mr. Becker. He will be remanded to the County Jail where he will be processed and stay awaiting a trial date. Miss Cora Williams and a prisoner by the name of Miss Ellie Fry have agreed to write out a statement about the horrors that took place in the Missouri State Penitentiary for Women during their confinement. That and the evidence submitted from the District Attorney's investigation has convinced me that Warden Becker can't be trusted to go the toilet by himself."

Cora breathed a sigh of relief. She wouldn't have to stand up and tell the court everything that happened to her. It would be beyond anything she'd ever encountered. With all that happened to Virgil, she didn't have the strength.

Gene McKinnon came into the courtroom with a dark complexioned man with hooded, dark eyes. "Your honor the court would like to call, Dominic Magana," John Osborn called out.

The man walked to the stand. More like the insolent swagger of a man used to a lot of attention, instead of testifying in a court of law. He was seated and sworn in. "Is your name Dominic Magana?"

"That's what my mama claims. They call me The Dom for short."

"We're not interested in nicknames, Mr. Magana."

He shrugged. "Whatever."

"You've been called here because you have information alleging that Judge Martin and Mr. Robert Williams are in business together. Business of an illegal nature."

"I can only say that *The Judge* and Williams have been doing business with the Gallo mob in Chicago for the last seven years."

"That's not true," Judge Martin shouted.

"Sure it is," Magana said calmly. "Here in St. Louis they traffic the drugs, prostitution, gambling, bootlegging and all the racketeering business." John braced his hand on the witness stand. "How do you know of their crimes, Mr. Magana?"

"I was the go between for them and my boss, Mr. Gallo. They ran everything out of the prison Becker was in charge of."

"So Warden Becker is involved?"

"Yeah, he has the biggest prostitution ring in the area. He used the inmates." Mr. Magana kissed his fingertips. "They made a fortune."

"How much money did these men make a year?"

"Woo, their cut was well over five mill, at least."

"And do have any proof of these alleged crimes?"

"I turned over the books I was able to get out of Chicago. There are numbers on every activity and Williams' and Martin's names are all over them."

"What do you know about the death of Eleanor Martin?"

Mr. Magana shrugged and leaned back, checking out his fingernails. "I didn't know much until I asked around a little. It seems the woman was a lot smarter than they gave her credit for. I heard she found some incriminating evidence and the old man clicked her."

"The old man? Who's that?"

"The Judge."

"Not Dan Martin?"

"Naw, the kid didn't do anything. He's got no balls."

John Osborn held up several notebooks. "Here are the books that will detail all the dealings between the Gallo family and Mr. Robert Williams and Judge Albert Martin. Including murder."

The defense attorneys had their heads together frantically talking. Cora surmised they were desperately trying to come up with something that would discredit Dominic Magana's testimony.

Finally, John returned to his seat and Mr. Stone stood to cross examine. "Do they have anything else, your honor? I mean those books could be fake. As desperate as this court is to impeach my clients, this could've all been made up."

The Dom leaned forward and banged his fist on the table. "Hey, it could be, but it ain't. If I was gonna lie, it'd be a helluva lot bigger than this bullshit."

The judge leaned forward. "This court reminds you to be respectful."

The defense attorney tugged on the bottom of his vest and asked, "Did you ever witness the two men do anything illegal?"

"Not in front of me."

"You ever overhear them talking?"

"No."

"So, really all we have is a man from Chicago who's probably been promised protection from the mob for testifying to something he's never seen or heard."

The judge offered the DA an opportunity to cross examine, but John declined, as he tapped his pencil on the table.

Judge Steinberg said, "We'll recess until this afternoon at one."

They all stood. Cora turned to Batcher. "What about my father? Is it true he's involved? What's next? This isn't looking promising."

"Not at this point. We've do have Martin on attempted murder. You father is in this up to his neck."

"Dear God, but there has to be more evidence."

"I'm afraid so."

Judge Garner stood nearby and encouraged Gene McKinnon, Batcher and her to move inside a room off to the side. As they all gathered, he closed the door and wandered across the room. "Cora, since most of the crimes were committed in the prison, do you remember anything? Did you see anything?"

"I'm trying to think. Virgil told me my father visited the warden but he never came to see me." She looked around, uncomfortably. "They used all of us for prostitution and there were some pretty well known members of St. Louis society who came regularly."

Gene took out his notepad. "Can you provide names?"

"Yes, a few."

"Anything else. Any place in the prison that was off limits?"

"There was a place, but I never knew what went on there. The warden entertained almost every night. All the prisoners knew there were drugs, gambling, drinking and all that stuff, but we weren't really involved in that."

"My guess is that's where the big stuff went down. What about your father. Have you any idea why he'd put you through all this? He had to know once you were released there was a chance you'd go to the authorities."

"I've been racking my brain for five years trying to figure that out. I thought, or maybe hoped, that someone was blackmailing him and he had no choice, but I know in my heart he did."

"We've got to find something on them and it has to stick."

She tapped her bottom lip, thinking. "Have you talked to a guard named Jim Duffer? He's one of the few decent men in there."

"We did and he actually gave the investigators the information and showed them the horrors going on there. He's the reason the place is being overhauled."

She tightened her mouth. "He may have been too nice for them to let him in on anything that might be used in a court of law." She snapped her fingers. "Did you talk to Grubber? He knows everything."

"Yeah, but they're paying him a lot of money to keep his mouth shut. He's not talking."

"Do you think he'd talk to me?" She looked at the judge. "Don't they have a lot of listening devices they used during the war?"

"There are things out there, but I doubt he'd talk because he knows we're desperate to find out something concrete we can hold Williams and Martin on."

Cora leaned against the wall. "At least now Eleanor's killer will go to jail. All this time I thought it was Dan."

"I think The Dom was right. Eleanor got too close to the truth and the judge decided it was too dangerous to let her live."

"But why would my father allow that to happen? I'm surprised he didn't kill Martin with his bare hands for murdering his daughter."

"That is strange. There has to be something there."

Cora walked toward the door. "I'm going to visit Virgil. I want to make sure he's still improving."

Batcher and McKinnon fell in behind her. "We'll go with you."

Cora didn't know if they were doing it to protect her or they wanted to check on their friend as well. Either way she was very grateful.

CHAPTER THIRTY-SEVEN

Virgil had just had a sponge bath and another needle jabbed into his arm for the pain. He'd be damned glad when he could stand up and get out of this place.

He couldn't help but wonder what was going on inside the courtroom and how Cora was holding up. What was happening and if Cora had rested last night. He'd been knocked out by drugs most of the time, but when he woke, he looked for her.

The door opened and he glanced up and saw Batcher and McKinnon accompanying Cora into the room. Holding his arms out to her, he smiled when she was finally in his embrace.

"So, how's it going?"

"They've got Martin on putting the hit out on you, so he'll stand trial for that. We also learned that he, and not Dan, murdered Eleanor because she knew too much."

Virgil squeezed Cora's hand. "I'm sorry."

"I know." She leaned down and kissed him. "What we're trying to figure out is why my father would let the judge get away with that?"

"Yeah, it's one thing to have your own little mob going, but quite another to let your partner murder your child."

McKinnon came closer. "Do you think the judge lied to him? Convinced Williams that Eleanor really did commit suicide?"

Virgil looked at Cora. "How upset was he over the death of Eleanor?"

"He and my mother were shocked. I remember when Judge Martin came to our house. He was very apologetic and concerned, but my parents seemed to accept what he said."

"Did you?"

"Not for a minute."

Batcher sat on the edge of the bed. "Why didn't you believe Martin's story?"

"I'd had lunch with Eleanor a few days before. She had been upset about something but she never said what."

"You didn't expect her to go home and days later commit suicide?"

"Absolutely not. She wouldn't do that to Jack."

Virgil took her hand. "Cora, think back to that conversation. What exactly did Eleanor say?"

"We talked about Jack." Cora looked away. "That's the day she told me she'd made me guardian of Jack should anything happen to her." Cora's hand flew to her mouth. "I forgot about that."

Virgil squeezed her hand. "Okay, did you find that unusual?"

"No, not really. We both consider Jack's grandparents too cold and uncaring."

Gene cocked his head. "Why not leave the boy with his father?"

Cora's brow wrinkled. "She was angry with Dan because he refused to move out of his parent's home and get them their own place. She said they had the money, but Judge Martin wanted his only child under his thumb."

Virgil asked, "Did she say anything else about the judge or your father?"

"Only that the two were inseparable. She also felt she and Dan were pawns in the scheme of things."

"Like how?" Batcher asked.

"She always referred to the two families coming together as a dynasty. Like now there was an unbreakable bond that held the two men even closer."

"What did their wives think?" Virgil asked. "Did they get along? Were they friends?"

"My mother never cared for Gloria Martin. The two never hit it off."

"Did Eleanor like her mother-in-law?"

"Eleanor couldn't stand Dan's parents. And she let that be known to both families."

Virgil sat up and tried to figure out why Cora's father would not only put her in prison for a crime she didn't commit but also overlook the murder of his other child. Just how calloused was the man? "I'm at a loss. I can't for the life of me put this case together."

Gene scratched his head. "Doesn't make a lot of sense. There has to be a reason this is all okay with Williams."

Batcher shook his head. "I don't even know who to question to find out the answers."

He looked at Cora and she asked, "How did Eleanor find out about the judge and our father being a part of the mob? What did she uncover? Did she have evidence? If so, where is it? Who did she tell and where does the truth lie?"

Virgil's expression suddenly tensed. "I think I've figured this all out and only one person can set the record straight."

Batcher and Gene glanced at Virgil. "Get me out of here. I need to talk to the District Attorney."

"But, you can't leave. If you start bleeding again, you could die," Cora pleaded.

He threw off the sheet. "Get my clothes, David." He looked at Cora. "You can either help me get dressed or go cover the door and make sure no one's coming."

"I'll get a wheelchair," Gene offered.

"Are you crazy?" she shouted.

"No, and I think I know who has all the answers and why. We need to get out of here."

They reached the courthouse and made it upstairs to the courtroom in time for Virgil, wearing only his trousers, the hospital gown and his coat draped over his shoulders, to speak at length with John Osborn and JJ.

He remained at the table when the judge came in. As difficult as it was, he managed to stand for the judge.

John stood. "The State calls Mrs. Clare Williams to the stand."

The attorney on the other side of the room jumped to his feet. "A woman can't be made to testify against her husband."

"She can be asked." John shrugged. "But we're not asking her to testify against her husband, your honor."

Much to Virgil's surprise, the judge allowed it and Clare Williams stood. Her face was calm and emotionless as she strolled to the stand like the whole matter was a waste of her time. After taking the oath, she stared at him.

"Mrs. Williams, how did you find out about the death of your daughter, Eleanor Martin?"

A long pause followed then she finally replied. "Judge Martin came to our home and told us."

"Did he say she'd committed suicide?"

"Yes, he did."

"Did you believe him?"

She looked surprised, as she took a moment to answer. Then she calmly replied. "I was stunned."

"Did you believe him?"

She looked away and lifted her chin. "I guess I did."

"But your daughter, Cora, didn't believe that story. Why did you?"

"Cora is high-strung and at times out-spoken."

"Yes, but she felt her sister had been murdered."

She glanced at her husband. "Robert told me Cora was hysterical and that what Judge Martin had said was true. Eleanor had killed herself."

"So, you knew nothing of the fiasco of the death certificate the judge forged or any of that?"

"I steer clear of gossip."

"I see, but after all, she was your daughter."

Clare Williams sent the District Attorney a scalding glare. "I'm clearly aware of that, sir."

"So, what did you think when your older daughter was sent to prison?"

She couldn't bring herself to look at Cora. "I found it very distasteful."

"No compassion for her and what you've heard she had to endure?"

Her eyes moved to Williams, who lowered his head. "Of course a mother has feelings when one of her children suffers."

"Yet, you didn't once pay your daughter a visit, send a letter, even question your husband when he returned from the very hellhole your daughter was being held."

"I never knew he went there and it distresses me greatly that he didn't put a stop to all of it."

"Does it annoy you enough to tell the truth?"

She clutched her purse tightly and lifted her chin. "I've been very cooperative and I've only spoken the truth."

"Okay, so your husband sends your daughter to prison, you disown her, and now you've learned that Judge Martin has been charged with murdering your younger daughter. Yet you have nothing to say?"

"What is there to say?"

"What about admitting that Cora is not Robert Williams' child?"

Cora's mother's breathing increased and she looked at the judge. "I have nothing further to say."

The judge stared down at her. "I've requested you to testify. Now it's up to you, but you'll sit there through the questioning."

"You didn't love Robert Williams when you married him did you?"

"I was fond of him."

"No you weren't. According to your best friend Alice Bishop, who still lives in your hometown, you detested the man."

"That's very strong language."

"You only married him because your father insisted on the marriage to get you away from Hiram Thompson who you were deeply in love with."

Robert Williams studied the floor.

"That's why he didn't mind putting the bastard child in prison. But why let Martin get away with killing Eleanor?"

Silence filled the room and Clare visibly struggled to bring herself under control. She snapped and unsnapped her purse, adjusted her coat, cleared her throat and nibbled her bottom lip.

Suddenly Clare Williams burst out laughing. "It's all a lie. I let him believe Cora wasn't his because that was my way of punishing him for not loving me the way Hiram did. Because Robert didn't have those kinds of feelings in him."

She stared at Cora. "She's as much his flesh and blood as Eleanor was. I thought it insane that he couldn't see how much she was like him. The stubbornness, the boldness, the way she went after things, how driven she was to succeed." Clare Williams looked at her husband. "You were such a fool."

Robert Williams looked at Cora, his eyes wide, his mouth open. He came to his feet and pointed to his wife. "You're lying."

"No, I'm not. It's the God's honest truth. You thought she was Hiram's child because you were always eager to believe the worst in people."

The judge pounded his gavel to quiet the room.

John stood in front of Clare Williams. "Back to Eleanor's death."

"Robert and Albert were in so thick with the Chicago mob they had no choice. If Eleanor didn't keep her mouth shut, they'd have to kill her."

"Do you know this to be true? Is there evidence?"

She reached inside her purse and pulled out a key. "This is to a safety deposit box that has years of records of every crime and vice the two men were involved in." She looked down. "Also, twenty years ago, Robert murdered a man in cold blood during a drunken brawl. Judge Martin made the whole thing go away. Robert had no choice but to let Martin do anything he wanted because he'd kept the evidence that would send him to the electric chair."

The two bailiffs grabbed Williams, handcuffed him and dragged him protesting out of court. Cora watched him, tears streaming down her cheeks. Surprisingly, when Clare Williams left the witness box her eyes were dry.

Cora went to Virgil and knelt down. "I can't believe my mother and father were so full of hate."

"It's often the case when you dip your toe into something shady. Before long, it consumes you. I think that's what happened to your parents."

As they walked out of the room a shot rang out. Virgil grabbed the wheels of the chair and they hurried toward the noise. Out in the hallway, Clare stood with a smoking gun in her hand, Judge Albert Martin lay dead on the stone floor.

She was quickly subdued and carried off to jail. Cora walked up to her father. "This is your entire fault. You've destroyed everything you've ever touched." She tapped her chest. "Except me and Jack. We're going to walk away from this completely unscathed and happy while you and the rest of your cronies rot in prison."

Virgil took her hand. "Let's go home. I'm sure Jack misses us." He looked up at Cora's emotionally untouched father. "I don't think I've met a more miserable human being. I'm glad you'll spend your life in jail. This way, Jack will never know about you."

Virgil turned to join Cora then looked back over his shoulder. "You want to know why your wife talked?"

Williams' gaze locked with his. "I told all her friends at the country club about your affair. I made sure she knew you'd

not only be unfaithful, but careless enough to embarrass her."
Virgil chuckled. "I knew she wouldn't tolerate that."

CHAPTER THIRTY-EIGHT

Cora sat on the couch in her house completely relaxed. Virgil was able to get around now and his wound was healing nicely. She'd insisted that he stay at her house and in bed until she deemed him ready to go back to light duty.

He'd been a horrible patient, but he followed her instructions and didn't overdo it. Other than a return trip to the hospital so a very unhappy Dr. Slater could sew up Virgil's wound again, they spent little time hurrying back home. His parents came to see him on several occasions during his recovery and she was happy to have them in her house. Especially since Virgil's father delighted spoiling Jack so much.

They'd returned from church, had lunch and were enjoying the quiet when Virgil left the bedroom and walked over to her. Holding on to the arm of the couch, he knelt down and held up a small, black box. Cora's heart burst from her chest.

He opened the lid exposing a beautiful ring. "I've asked you a dozen times to marry me and while you keep stalling, I think the least you can do is wear an engagement ring."

She placed her hands on her beating heart. "Really?"

"I want you to be my wife."

"But..."

"I don't want to hear any buts. You need to make an honest man out of me." He grinned. "Just say yes and let's set a date."

She patted the cushion next to her. Jack was at Tommy's so she knew now was the time to come clean about her past. If afterwards Virgil decided he didn't want any part of her, she'd try to understand.

"I want to tell you everything."

He put his hand on her cheek. "I don't need to know."

"I don't want any more secrets between us."

He nodded.

"You know I was prostituted out while I was in prison."

"That doesn't matter."

"The rest might."

"Go on."

"Almost every night there were men and guards and we did things I still can't describe in detail. They were horrible and I want you to know that I fought for the longest time. I took the beatings, the starving, the coffin, the ice showers, everything they threw at me."

He took her hand. "I know that had to be hard."

"Finally one day Ellie Fry came to me and told me that the warden has passed down orders that if I didn't do what I was told, the guards were to kill me that night."

"The bastards."

"She talked to me for a long time. Told me how to go in my mind to another place. How to just lay there and let them do whatever they wanted because someday it would end and I'd be a free woman again."

He cupped her chin. "I'm glad you stayed alive. I know it was horrible for you, but now you have me and Jack."

Tears coursed down her cheeks. "That's not the worst of it, Virgil."

"Tell me, Cora."

"When you know the whole truth, I expect you to walk away and I want you to know that it's okay."

"Don't say that. I won't."

"Virgil, I know you want a family. I know it means a great deal to you and I'd love to give you children." She whisked the tears from her face. "While I was in prison I became pregnant three different times."

"What?"

"There were three babies. But the doctor in the prison performed three abortions. The babies were murdered and I had no say in the matter. They tied me down and cut the fetus out of me while I screamed my head off."

She saw the horror well up in his eyes. "My God."

"That's why I can never have your children, Virgil. There is so much scar tissue and damage from the botched abortions that I can't ever conceive again." He reached out for her. She moved away and stood. "I don't know that I can be a decent wife after all I've been through."

"Cora, none of this was your fault."

"No, but it happened. That's why I can't take your ring. Go find someone who you can really love and admire. A woman who can offer you a family and all the things you deserve."

"Cora, I love you."

"What do you think the people of this town would think of me if they knew?"

"That doesn't matter."

"It does. I've been offered and accepted a job at St. Louis Memorial. Jack and I leave next weekend. Perhaps there we can build a new life."

"So, you knew this all along?"

She looked down at her hands. "I'd planned to tell you when we first came back, but..."

"No, you decided your whole future and didn't give me a second thought?"

"I did think of you, Virgil. That's why I'm leaving."

"You're leaving because you're a damned coward. You're like your father. You're too damned stubborn and selfish to love anyone. It's easier for you to just walk away." He picked up his coat. "Then go. If you don't have enough faith in me to know that I'd never, ever stop loving you, then it's best you run back to St. Louis. Go hide somewhere it's safe."

He left and slammed the door in his wake. Cora ran to the door and screamed for him to come back, but he was already in his squad car driving away.

Cora crumpled to the floor and cried until no more tears would fall.

She woke up later in the day to Maggie leaning over her, concern drawing her features tight. "What's wrong?"

"I told Virgil we were leaving."

Maggie frowned. "You're such a fool."

"Who's leaving," Jack asked.

Cora slowly got up and walked over and took the young boy into her arms. "Darling, I've been meaning to talk to you. Next week you and I are going on a bus ride to St. Louis."

Jack wiggled out of her grasp. "You just got back from there."

"I know, sweetheart, but this time we're going to live there in a nice big house." She tried to sound cheerful while misery filled her throat. "We might buy us a car."

Jack backed away. "I don't want to leave Tommy or Ronnie." He looked around. "Where is Uncle Virgil? Is he going with us?"

"No dear, he's staying here."

"Then I ain't going. I'm staying here with Uncle Virgil."

"You can't. This is really for the best."

Maggie folded her arms. "Good luck with that bull crap."

Cora wiped her face. "Jack we can work all this out once we get to St. Louis. You'll love living there."

His little fists balled in defiance. "I like it here."

"It will all work out."

Jack turned, ran for the front door and darted down the street. She stepped on the porch calling his name. He'd headed downtown toward the town square.

Maggie approached and wrapped Cora in her arms. "Cora, give the boy time. You're uprooting the only happy life he's ever known."

Exhausted and weary she looked up at Maggie. "Tell me I'm doing the right thing."

"I can't."

CHAPTER THIRTY-NINE

Virgil sat at his desk while the box holding the engagement ring mocked him. He'd been a damned fool to think he could ever break through Cora's hard shell and reach the real woman inside.

She'd built a wall ten feet high and three feet thick of brick and mortar that no mortal would ever penetrate. It was obvious to him that she didn't want to love anyone or anyone to love her. She was content to dwell in her miserable past so she had an excuse for not putting her heart out there.

It was a good thing that she was moving away. He didn't want to be running into her every time he turned around. In St. Louis, she'd be long gone and she could take all those memories with her.

He battled back tears. He'd stop loving her eventually. It might take years, but one day the right person would come along and maybe he'd be happy. The whole scenario was doubtful, but a man had to have hope.

God, he missed her already.

He heard someone pounding on the office door and he was tempted to ignore it until he heard Jack calling. Virgil stood and opened the door. The young boy threw his arms around Virgil's waist and cried. "I'm not leaving you. I won't go."

Fighting his own tears, Virgil picked up the child he considered his own son. Jack. He hadn't considered what this would do to him.

Rubbing his back, Virgil crooned, "Now, don't get upset, Jack. Nothing's happened yet."

His face was red and wet with tears. The boy looked up at him. "Can you talk her into staying? Please, please, Uncle Virgil."

"I've tried, buddy. I really did."

"Then can I live with you?"

"I don't think that's possible." He sat Jack on this desk. "Your Aunt Cora needs you with her."

"But I want you."

"You just think you do."

The door opened and Cora walked in. Jack hid his face in the front of Virgil's shirt. "Make her go away, Uncle Virgil. Tell her we don't want her."

Virgil lowered his head. "I can't do that, son."

"Let's go home," she said with a shaky voice.

"This is my home. I'm not going with you."

"Now, Jack. You watch the way you talk to her. Don't be disrespectful."

"I'm not, but she don't care nothing about us. She's going to move to St. Louis and she doesn't care how much it hurts us."

"I think she cares."

"No," Jack shouted. "She don't know or she wouldn't do it."

Tears streamed down Cora's face. "I'm sorry, Jack."

The young boy buried his face in Virgil's chest and cried, his little shoulders moving up and down and he wept until Virgil couldn't help but join him.

The door quietly closed and, when Virgil looked around, Cora was gone and he and Jack were left with their pain and loneliness. Soon, he was able to wash Jack's face and get him to Betty's Diner for a burger, but neither talked. After finishing their meal, they returned to the station.

Soon, darkness crept over the town and Jack finally fell into an exhausted sleep. Virgil wrapped him up in a blanket and put him in the squad car to take him home.

Cora opened the door and allowed him to tuck Jack into bed for the last time. He sat next to the little boy, holding his tiny hand and wondered about the kind of man he'd become. With tears in his eyes he prayed that Jack would never fight a war, never take another man's life, and never get his heart broken.

It was hard to think of life without the little boy. He'd miss teaching him to fish, hunt, drive a car, feel the pride of watching Jack hit a homerun, watch him graduate from school and grow into a strong, young man. One he'd be proud to call son. None of that was in Virgil's future. Just the memory of a little boy so desperate for love he reached out with his heart and both hands.

Virgil stood and walked past Cora without saying a word, shutting the door in his wake. He refused to cry in front of her anymore.

CHAPTER FORTY

By Wednesday, Cora was so miserable she felt like admitting herself into the hospital for psychological care. Jack refused to speak to her, Maggie wasn't all that friendly, Earl ignored any attempt she made at trying to communicate with him, and her heart ached so badly she honestly wanted to die.

Every angry word Virgil had spoken to her Sunday still pierced her heart like a dagger. Looking at everything, she realized she was being selfish and afraid to love. Scared and foolish, but what could she do?

Dr. Lowery came into her office. "I was wondering if you'd had lunch yet."

"I'm not really hungry."

He took a seat. "I know you're facing a very challenging moment in your life, Cora, and I wish I had some words of wisdom, but I don't. All I can say is do what your heart tells you."

She chuckled. "If I did that I'd go to Virgil's office throw myself at his feet and beg him to take me back."

"And what would be so bad about that if you really love him."

"I do love him, but I guess the way my father treated me has left me insecure and unable to trust."

"Is that Virgil's fault?"

"No, of course not. But, unfortunately he's suffered the worst of it. I say that, but still I sit here so broken hearted myself that I can barely breathe."

"Maybe it's time the two of you talked."

"Oh, we're way past talking. I doubt Virgil will ever say another word to me."

"You never know." He stood to leave. "If you should decide to stay, your job's always here."

"Thank you so much for that. I appreciate all you've done."

Cora left work early and decided she needed to go home to lie down and hopefully get rid of the headache she'd been carrying around for three days. Walking into her home only reminded her of Virgil and how much she loved him.

After trying to take a nap and not being able to close her eyes, Cora sat up, washed her face and put her coat on to go get Jack and Tommy from school. On the way there, she'd thought about stopping by and seeing if Virgil would talk to her, but decided she'd pick up the boys then later she and Jack would walk to the station. Better yet, maybe she could leave Jack with Maggie and go alone.

When she arrived at school the boys were just getting out and Jack and Tommy both had long, unhappy faces. "Hello boys, how was school?"

"Fine."

Not another word. As they turned onto Liberty Street, a brand new Ford pulled up to the curb and a man got out of the car. Cora froze. Dan Martin walked toward her. Instinctively, she put the boys behind her. "What do you want?"

"I thought I'd see Jack before I go away."

"No," Cora hissed. "Go away."

"Who's that, Aunt Cora?"

"No one." She stepped back. "Get in your car and leave now."

"He's my son. I can take him anytime I want to."

Suddenly Virgil pulled up in the squad car, jumped out and grabbed Dan by the arm. "Boys, head on to Tommy's house. Aunt Cora and I will be there soon."

Without another word the boys ran toward Maggie's as Cora trembled in fear. "He's here to see Jack."

"You're out on bail, Martin. You're not allowed in my county."

"I just came to see my kid before my trial."

"You don't have a kid. You're going to jail. Tomorrow morning, I'll have the sheriff from Carthage escort you back to St. Louis where your bail will be revoked."

Martin tried to break free, but Virgil had him in a tight grip and the handcuffs on before Dan could do much of anything. Virgil shoved him into the back seat.

"He just came up on us." Cora put her hands on her chest. "He scared me to death."

"I'll take him in and notify Carthage to come and get him immediately."

"I don't want Jack to see him."

"He won't."

Cora covered her face and tears flowed. "This is all so crazy." She grabbed Virgil by the shirt. "Please help me make sense of it all. Please take the pain away and please love me."

He wrapped his arms around her and every ounce of anguish slipped from her body and she grew limp. Still he continued to hold her. "I love you," she whispered. "I have since the moment I saw you. I was afraid and scared, but something inside me came back to life the second I laid eyes on you."

"I love you, too," Virgil said. "But, I'm afraid of losing you."

Cora looked up at him and smiled through the tears. "I'm not going anywhere, I promise."

"Good, I didn't really want to move to St. Louis."

CHAPTER FORTY-ONE

The weather was miserable, Ethan had dropped the boxed cake running up the stairs, and one of the heels broke off her shoe, but Cora couldn't be happier.

Her wedding day would be one to remember. In the judge's chambers, filled with all their friends and Virgil's family, she waited out in the hall with Earl, all decked out in a fancy suit, to walk her down the aisle.

Maggie was her maid of honor and Jack and Tommy had been tossing tissue flowers all over the place acting silly. Cora's face hurt from smiling so much.

"I'm awfully glad you came to your senses. I liked to have never talked Chesterfield out of giving you that job in St. Louis."

"What?"

"He was going to call you as soon as you got Jack home from school."

"But Dan interrupted that?"

"And you two had kissed and made up."

"Earl, you're quite the manipulator."

"Guess I am. I got you two together, didn't I?"

The door opened and Virgil stood in the front of the room in a nicely tailored suit, shiny, black shoes and a smile that matched hers. Earl walked her slowly toward him, the hem of

208

her dress barely touching the floor. Of course, she walked on one tiptoe to stay even.

With a kiss on the cheek, Earl put her hand in Virgil's. She looked into his blue eyes and saw a love so true it cleared away all the past and promised a bright future.

Turning to the judge, they both said their "I dos" and then Virgil kissed her amid cheering, laughter and clapping. When they separated and turned to their friends and family. Judge Francis Garner said, "There's nothing in this world that gives me greater pleasure than to introduce you to the new Mr. and Mrs. Virgil Carter."

Everyone applauded and Virgil kissed her again. "I love you so much," he said.

"I love you too."

"I promise to always be the man you love."

"I promise I'll be the woman you deserve."

He kissed her deeply and completely.

Jack tugged at her dress. "You know, that kiss was probably worth a dime."

Tommy shook his head. "She's losing money every day."

"I know," Jack said with a troubled expression. "She gives him free kisses all the time."

"I want to find me a girl that gives free kisses," little Ronnie said. "Cause I think free kisses are the bestest ones."

GERI FOSTER

BOOKS BY GERI FOSTER

THE FALCON SECURITIES SERIES
OUT OF THE DARK
WWW.AMAZON.COM/DP/B00CB8GY9K

OUT OF THE SHADOWS
WWW.AMAZON.COM/DP/B00CB4QY8U

OUT OF THE NIGHT
WWW.AMAZON.COM/DP/BOOF1F7Q9M

OUT OF THE PAST
WWW.AMAZON.COM/DP/BOOJSVTRVU

ACCIDENTAL PLEASURES SERIES

WRONG ROOM
WWW.AMAZON.COM/DP/B00GM9PU94
WRONG BRIDE
WWW.AMAZON.COM/DP/B00NOZMNSU
WRONG PLAN
WWW.AMAZON.COM/DP/B00MO2RFR8
WRONG HOLLY
WWW.AMAZON.COM/DP/B00OBS03M2
WRONG GUY
WWW.AMAZON.COM/DP/B00KK94F6G

ABOUT THE AUTHOR

As long as she can remember, Geri Foster has been a lover of reading and the written words. In the seventh grade she wore out two library cards and had read every book in her age area of the library. After raising a family and saying good-bye to the corporate world, she tried her hand at writing.

Action, intrigue, danger and sultry romance drew her like a magnet. That's why she has no choice but to write action-romance suspense. While she reads every genre under the sun, she's always been drawn to guns, bombs and fighting men. Secrecy and suspense move her to write edgy stories about daring and honorable heroes who manage against all odds to end up with their one true love.

You can contact Geri Foster at geri.foster@att.net

Printed in Great Britain
by Amazon.co.uk, Ltd.,
Marston Gate.